Snow and Mistletoe

AN EASTON FAMILY CHRISTMAS

JEN GEIGLE JOHNSON

Follow Jen

Some of Jen's other published works:

The Nobleman's Daughter
Two lovers in disguise

A Lady's Maid
A dual romance, the struggle continues

Scarlet
The Pimpernel retold

His Lady in Hiding
Hiding out at his maid.

A Foreign Crown
A Lady in Waiting meets a Prince

Spun of Gold
Rumplestilskin Retold

Dating the Duke

Time Travel: Regency man in NYC

Tabitha's Folly
Four over protective Brothers

To read Damen's Secret
The Villain's Romance

Charmed by His Lordship
A fake alliance

Follow her Newsletter

Chapter One

L ately, things were odd. Her mother hadn't left her bedroom in two weeks. Her father entertained untitled people from all walks of life. The servants were skittish. But no one would say anything at all about why.

Lady Theadosia Manet sat pondering the oddities with a book in hand, passing the time before calling hours. She'd like to be finishing her book. Another of Jane Austen's had just been published, and she had to finish the one in hand before she could begin the other. But the pages to her latest gothic novel were left unturned as her mind puzzled their situation. Could Father be working on another bill for Parliament? Could he be doing research? Could he be aiding the Bow Street Runners as he was sometimes wont? A maid bobbed a curtsey in front of her. "Your father would like to see you in his study."

Something in her throat tightened. A summons to Father's study usually meant pleasant conversation, but today the feelings of dread were surprising at the same time they were expected. Perhaps she could learn something that would explain their staying in London for Christmas, or the fact that her father didn't go to White's anymore, but stayed locked up in his study, receiving caller after caller.

She made her way through the rooms at the front of their home. Her fingers trailed on the backs of their furniture. Would things start to make sense around their home again? As soon as she entered the study, and Father looked as though he'd been up all night, nothing on his tea tray touched, she knew things were about to become even more strange. "What is it?"

He glanced up from what looked to be a well-read letter, the folds growing worn. "Come in. Sit."

She did, but only just. Her backside barely covered the corner of the chair, her legs poised to rise.

While dipping his pen in ink, he began. "Lord Standish has asked for your hand."

She nearly spit in surprise. "In marriage?"

"Yes, Dosie." His neat hand penned more words. "That's generally what asking for a hand entails."

"Was he overly disappointed when you refused?"

Father didn't meet her eyes.

"You did refuse him, didn't you?"

"Not…precisely." He finally looked up from his work.

"Father, you must do so, and sooner rather than later. I can't have the man thinking he can come call, follow me about at the balls and such."

"I'm not certain refusing him is the best decision."

"How can you say that? Would *you* want to live with him? He's as pale as the dead. He…he looks unhappy all the time. The man scowls." She shivered.

"Hardly reasons to dismiss him outright."

She couldn't believe the words that were entering her ears. Dosie shook her head. "I will turn him down." But her father kept talking.

"We could do really well by him."

"We could do well by him?" She repeated her father's

words hoping he would see how he sounded. Was he speaking of an offer of marriage or a business arrangement? Obviously the latter. "I feel cold whenever he's near. Real gooseflesh and not the pleasant kind."

"The weather has been…drafty."

"No Father, that's not it. He's…not a good man."

"He might be lovely. You don't know him very well."

"But I know him well enough. Father. What is this talk? We do not need to marry in haste. We can be selective, can't we? I don't wish to marry yet, and I certainly don't wish to marry him." She stood to emphasize her point, hoping her father would listen. "I will turn him down."

Her father's eyes, though resigned, held a certain glint to them and she wondered what the hurry was and why Lord Standish? Why this dreadful man of all the men?

"He is persuasive, that is all." Her father closed his ledger. "He comes to me with an offer I find difficult to refuse. He's extraordinarily connected, you know."

"With whom?" The man was an earl.

"His father will be appointed as the newest duke. He's meeting with Prinny this month. Lord Standish will soon be the most sought-after man in all of London, and you will have already captured him."

"And this new duke?"

"He's key to the balance of votes in Parliament. He is believed to be a Whig."

She stopped caring the minute votes and Parliament entered the discussion. But she knew her father had carefully drafted and argued and wrote papers on certain bills and efforts he hoped to move forward in the House of Lords and Commons. He was very active and cared deeply about his position there, sometimes to the exclusion of all else.

But he rubbed his forehead in resignation. "We will speak no more about it today."

"Have you been working on a bill lately? You've been so…distracted."

"Yes. Perhaps one of the most important of our day. It is coming together, remarkably, miraculously. But I need all the votes I can muster, all the assistance." He sighed. "I haven't even seen your mother these past weeks."

A servant scratched at the door.

"Come." Her father's voice sounded tired.

A maid entered with a curtsey. "Lady Theadosia has callers, my lord."

"Is it that time already?" She stood. "Thank you, Father. I really do wish to assist you in your pursuits. This must be of the utmost importance if you were to ask a marriage of me." She waited. But he was distracted once more, taking his quill up again. He looked up as if just remembering her presence. "Thank you. Enjoy your callers. The man himself is likely warming your front room furniture with all his coldness."

A certain growing concern stayed with her as she left his study and moved to the front room to receive callers. With any luck, Lady Jane would have already arrived.

She stood at the opened double doors to their front receiving parlor. Just as her father predicted, Lord Standish's dark presence had descended, and did she imagine things or did the temperature in the room drop? She shivered.

The footman announced, "Lady Theadosia Manet."

Everyone stood: two lords she quite enjoyed, her dear Lady Jane, and the ominous Lord Standish. She curtseyed, smiling at the room at large, avoiding looking too closely or deeply at Lord Standish.

Lady Jane gave her a look, the kind of look that meant, *oh I have things to say but I cannot say them.* And Dosie wished immediately that they were alone. But instead, she had the shy Lord Denning making eyes in her direction; the effervescent Lord Hamilton fanning his face; and the eerie Lord Standish sulking in the corner, so to speak. Hopefully she and Lady

Jane would manage without Dosie's mother who had complained earlier of the nerves. What precisely were the nerves? Dosie had yet to learn. But her mother had them and therefore it was up to Dosie and Lady Jane to make the best of things.

Dosie began by pouring tea. "Tell me, Lord Denning. How is your mother?"

"Oh, she is well." He nodded four times before continuing. "Well indeed."

"Excellent, and Lord Hamilton."

"Hm?"

"I am admiring your cravat from here. Is that a pattern I see in the folds?"

He lifted his chin. "Yes, you are the first to comment." He eyed the men on either side before continuing. "The fabric itself has been stamped with ducks. It reminds me of the Hamilton hunt that happens every year at our house party. You will be attending, will you not?" He looked most specifically at Lady Jane, which Dosie found amusing. She liked Lord Hamilton. And she would be pleased if he could find a good match. Lady Jane would be highly entertained by him all her days. Wouldn't be the worst match. Unlike Lord Standish, who would undoubtedly be the worst match as far as overall congeniality.

"We are attending." Dosie nodded. "Will you also be attending, Lord Denning?"

He bumbled for a moment, looking this way and that until at last he said, "Yes."

Lord Standish shifted in his seat. "I, too, shall be attending. Although, I wonder if I might see you, Lady Theadosia, at the ball tonight?"

"Is there a ball tonight?" She tapped her chin, although she knew very well that there was indeed a ball, one she most desperately wished to attend, one that she and Lady Jane had been discussing for weeks.

"Quite. The Dansford ball." His expression remained placid, intense yet at the same time bored looking. How he managed such a feat was beyond her, but the result was unnerving.

"Oh yes, the very one. Yes. We will both be attending."

He opened his mouth to ask for her first set. She could see it on his lips, hear the words before they were uttered. She pinched Lady Jane.

"Lord Standish!" Her voice, blurting though it was, had the desired effect. He turned his attention to her. She started for a moment as though at a loss for words. Lord Standish had that effect with his tall, overly thin frame and his long pointed nose. The pallor of his skin, though much admired in the ladies, gave him an ethereal effect. He belonged in a gothic novel. But despite all of that raven-like eeriness looking down upon her, Lady Jane rallied. "Um. You see. I was wondering if you had heard any news from your sister?"

Remarkable. What a glorious friend Lady Jane was. His sister had moved to India with her new husband. Excellent conversation. Safe as well.

And as predicted, he talked for many minutes about India, about the heat, the animals, the smells and how his sister was doing everything she could not to brown her skin. But to no avail, apparently she was particularly freckled.

"There's no need for a person to become weathered." Lord Hamilton shuddered.

"Well now, perhaps I am a bit of a different duck, but I do think some sun on the cheeks can add something to a complexion, no?" Dosie looked to Lady Jane for her support but she shook her head. "Not this Lady. I don't get a lovely pink rouge. I freckle. And they are impossible to lose."

Lord Standish continued. "She says the monkeys are adorable. She hopes to bring one home to London when they return and that the food is delicious, especially the fruits."

They talked for many minutes on the lack of fruit in

London this season and then the hours for calling had come to a close. Lady Jane and Lady Theadosia stood. "Thank you for coming." Lady Theadosia offered her hand to each as they moved past toward the door. Lord Standish waited a moment before he approached, presumably so that fewer were in the room. "I would like to beg your hand for the first set of the dance."

"Of course." She curtseyed. "Thank you for coming today."

He stepped closer and lowered his voice. "Perhaps your father has spoken to you?" His eyebrow rose, but in his case the effect was so much less appealing and more of a demanding sort of question that Lady Theadosia wanted nothing more than to deny any conversation had taken place.

But honesty prevailed. "Yes, we have spoken."

"I look forward to spending more time at your side."

She held up a hand. "Before you say more, you must know that I have not accepted a courtship, nor any other more formal arrangement. I am much more comfortable leaving such things undecided for now."

His mouth straightened into a line, and Lady Jane shivered beside her. At least Dosie wasn't the only one to be so affected by this rather singularly unappealing man. But he bowed and said only, "I look forward to our set."

"Thank you."

He left, but the coldness that oft travelled in his wake lingered.

Chapter Two

Julian Easton studied the odds of all the horses about to race. Cherry Picker was widely considered the first choice to win. Which meant he was going to bet against her. Everyone knew that you could win big doing things that way. And Cherry Picker couldn't win every single race of the day. It just wasn't possible. He put everything in his pocket down on the horse most predicted to lose. Nodded, satisfied with his potential, he made his way to the stands to watch the races.

Tauney had come, but only because Julian had forced him to. The man had no interest in wagers, betting, horse races or gambling in any way. Which Julian found odd. But he was the best of brothers and the only one who had nothing else to do.

"I think you have good odds with Cherry Picker."

"I didn't bet on her."

"What? Why not? I thought we were coming here because she was the one horse who couldn't lose? Everyone says it. Guaranteed return so you can pay back Edward?" Tauney's expression filled Julian with doubts about his last-minute rash decision.

"Look, I know what I'm doing. I've been studying this stuff for weeks."

"And losing for weeks."

"Not today." He shook his head. "I feel good about this."

"Do I want to know who you bet on?"

He shook his head. "Bad luck. I'll tell you when he wins."

Tauney flicked a piece of dust from his jacket. "I don't know how this place is always so dirty."

Julian shrugged. He never minded a bit of dirt. He'd enjoy working on the estate if they were home. London life was confining for him. But the races made up for that.

The gun fire started the first race. Julian's horse wouldn't come up until the fourth. "You ever going to marry, Tauney?"

"If Edward has anything to do with it, I will."

"He's like...what is he like? I've never seen a brother harp on his siblings so much."

"I think he means for us to be happy." Tauney grimaced.

"Hmm."

They sat in silence for a minute, cheering or moans of disappointment as their backdrop. Then Tauney turned to him. "I'll marry. I'd like a family."

"Me too, someday." Julian did wish to marry, but with what? Where would he live? On what money? Perhaps these gambling ventures would pay off at last and he could start putting money down on an estate. "I'd like to be a landholder."

"Would you?" Tauney's raised eyebrows raised so much doubt that Julian had to call him on it. "You don't believe me?"

"I believe you. But you throw away a lot of money for one who wants to buy an estate."

"I'm trying to win it back. I've just got to pay off Edward and some creditors and then I'm free and clear to put the funds aside. I'd like to live near the Easton estate."

Tauney nodded. "Excellent idea."

The announcer called, "Cherry Picker. Running Sands." The other names meant nothing. This was the race. Julian leaned forward.

"Is your horse in this race?"

He nodded.

The gun went off and the horses broke out onto the racetrack. At first Cherry Picker was in the lead. She'd been racing ahead and staying ahead for every race of the day. And it looked like she might do the same again. Julian clenched his fists.

But then Running Sands started to pick up the pace. He gained ground, passing one horse after another. One lap to go and he was still passing the others one at a time until they were in the finishing stretch and he was gaining on Cherry Picker.

Everyone in the stands stood. Julian bit the inside of his mouth. But then he couldn't resist. "Come on Running Sands!!" He shouted.

Tauney looked at him with mouth open. "You bet on Running Sands?"

"Yes, and look at him!"

The horse ran faster and closer, catching up until it was even with Cherry Picker, who was in the clear lead. At last, with barely a second to spare, Running Sands broke ahead and they crossed the finish line.

Julian jumped up and down. Tauney sat back, seemingly stunned. Everyone else in the stands fell back in a dejected heap. If no one else bet on Running Sands, Julian had won big, indeed.

"Today is my lucky day, Tauney. That's enough to get me started."

He clapped Julian on the back. "You, brother, are one lucky gentleman."

He chuckled as he made his way down to the betting boxes. He really had won big. He could win even bigger. This money would pay off his creditors, sure, but wouldn't put him ahead in saving for an estate. Perhaps he should try a little more of his luck.

Instead of cashing in his winnings, Julian turned it back in to bet on Running Sands again in his next race.

Humming, he returned to his seat.

"How much?" Tauney leaned close.

"Nearly two thousand pounds."

"What! That's incredible."

"I know. Watch it triple. I put it all up on Running Sands for his next race."

"You did what!" Tauney stood, his face equal parts shock and anger.

"Like I said, I've been doing this a long time."

Tauney didn't say anything more but he was clearly unhappy.

Race after race, they talked of small unimportant things until the last race of the day. Running Sands was up against the other winners from earlier races.

"Here we go. Tauney this is where you see the Julian magic."

At the gun, the horses tore out of their boxes. Running Sands took up the last spot. And Julian waited for him to start overtaking horses like he had earlier. He waited for one lap, then two, then three. "Come on, Running Sands!"

But the horse fell further behind for one lap, two, then three. And Julian knew he'd made the biggest gambling mistake of his life.

Not wanting to look at Tauney, he closed his eyes and listened to the announcer call the winner—not Running Sands. He couldn't say easy come easy go. He couldn't feel fine about it. A great feeling of waste descended. What was he doing here in the first place?

"What an incredible waste of time." Julian stood. "Come on, Tauney. Sorry I made you witness that."

Tauney said nothing but followed his brother through the stands and outside of the racing grounds.

The happy faces of people counting money surrounded him, but he pushed through it. "I've got to stop this."

Tauney's hand on his shoulder said more than any word could. It was there supporting, forgiving, even condemning with love—and Julian especially appreciated all of the words not spoken. Surely he would hear all those words later from Edward's mouth.

They stopped at White's, mostly to avoid returning home to Edward who no doubt had already heard or would hear of Julian's incredible waste of money.

The men's club was crowded, more so than usual. Perhaps Julian had made some money on his bets in the book. Every little bit helped at this point.

But it took almost a quarter hour to get a look at the book. Something must be going on of great interest in the ton. When at last he opened its pages, he saw his friend Lady Theadosia's name. And her father. He was trying to push forward a Whig agenda. People were betting who the woman would marry. Everyone picked a Whig supporter, someone of influence in the Parliament, or other such type. Julian shook his head. If Lady Theadosia had anything to say about it, and knowing her as he did, she would have much to say, she wouldn't be marrying a single one of the cads on that list. They'd met as children, their families often taking dinner together, and had become fast friends. She was singularly the most independently minded woman of his acquaintance.

He turned to Tauney. But he'd lost his brother.

Beau Brummell himself had just entered the club. Tauney gravitated to him like most of the others and would be listening to every word for as long as the fashion paragon chose to stay and speak.

Julian found a place in the corner. Perhaps he should alert

Lady Theadosia that she and her father's dealings were so openly discussed.

Lord Standish entered. Julian knew very little of him, but he drew the eye. A bit odd in the manner of his dress but more especially in that the man never smiled. Julian nodded in his direction and received barely a tip of the head in return.

Several other lords joined Julian and with the great fuss over Beau Brummell, no one paid any attention to Lord Standish and his group. But one of the men slipped some coin, a full bag by the looks of it, into Standish's hands.

Keenly interested in any passage of coin, Julian pondered their small group for many minutes. Certainly no good was coming of their goings on. But coin. Julian could use some coin. He was about to stand and make his way over to them when Tauney laughed overly loud.

Their group of fashion frenzied men would be going on for many hours. And Standish and his group had already slipped away when he turned back to them. He sighed. No other table held anyone of interest to him, and he had no desire to learn the latest knot for his cravat. It was time for him to make his way home.

Tauney nodded to his brother's farewell.

Julian stepped outside onto St. James Street with no particular direction and not feeling especially motivated to try to think of one.

Chapter Three

❧

As soon as Lord Standish had gone from her house, Dosie moved to shut the door to their front parlor, and she and Lady Jane collapsed on a sofa together. "That was rather difficult, was it not?"

"Somewhat? I think I would have preferred my mother had been present to monitor topics and things, but we held ourselves well, did we not?"

"We did indeed." Lady Jane sat up. "But what is Lord Standish talking about? What conversation with your father?"

When Dosie had related the lot of it to her best friend, Lady Jane sat silent for many moments. "Can he want you to marry someone simply for their connection to a duke?"

"Not just a connection. The man himself will be a duke when his father dies. I would be a Duchess." Dosie sighed. She cared not a whit about such things, especially when they included a lifetime with a man she couldn't respect. "Father is not demanding that I do. But he is asking me to consider, yes. Parliamentary matters are important to my father."

"Apparently so." Lady Jane sat back again. "But you cannot marry him."

"I will not. Have no fear. We must both marry the most

congenial and lovely lords so that when we pay visits, everyone will enjoy equally well." Dosie imagined years of time with her best friend and the thought eased any concern she might have about finding and marrying. At least she would have Lady Jane.

"And now we must plan again our entrance to the ball."

"Yes, you'll be at my side?"

"And we shall have coordinated gowns. Wear your sapphires."

"Oh yes, you as well." They sat together planning out every detail of the ball that was to be the best and biggest of the season. When they'd exhausted every possible detail, Lady Jane said what was perhaps most on either of their minds. "Do you suppose we shall meet our husbands?"

"I most certainly hope not, not at this first ball."

"I don't know. I shouldn't mind meeting him. Perhaps we don't immediately court, but he sees me and I him and we show that bit of interest." She smiled, dreamy and ridiculous, and Dosie shook her head. "That is the surest way to waste the rest of your season, make no mistake."

"And why is that?"

"Because the mystery is gone. The intrigue, the chase, the hunt, all of it gone, replaced by an exchange of doe eyed nonsense that continues through the season until one or the other is brave enough to do something about it. Where is the fun in that?"

Lady Jane, looking somewhat affronted, shook her head. "I thought that was the fun."

"Hm." Perhaps she was correct. "I have an aversion to the courting part of this Season. I wish to stay blissfully unattached at least until I have met and flirted with ten men."

"Ten!"

"Certainly, and why not? That would happen in one ball's time."

"But flirted! You might be considered...a flirt." Her friend's aghast expression made Dosie laugh.

"As I should be, were I to be flirting." She waited for her friend to grasp the obviousness of her statement, but it was lost as she now seemed to be troubled and bothered and would commence discussing the merits of finding one's husband. She could see the conversation formulating in her eyes.

Dosie hoped to marry just as much as Lady Jane. She just didn't want to rush into the decision, and she certainly did not want to commit herself to Lord Standish. If she acquainted herself with more men, she might choose more carefully, or so she thought.

Dosie stood. "At any rate, perhaps we shall take our walk in the park?"

"Oh yes, yes, good idea."

After the calling hours, many who lived right along Grosvenor Square could be seen out passing the time on the many paths of Hyde Park. And they wished to be seen walking with someone of influence. To see and be seen was the purpose of every promenade.

Dosie called to her butler. "Hansen."

"Yes, my lady."

"We require a maid and footman to accompany us to the park."

"Yes, my lady."

Soon they were out promenading with what felt like half the ton. And after a moment of smiling and nodding to people she did not know, Dosie saw little point in it. "Surely there is something more to do here than this."

"I think promenading is much better when you happen upon someone you know. We need more introductions."

"Too true." They studied a group of women and men laughing and carrying on as if they hadn't seen each other for the whole of summer and now into fall. "What will happen this spring when there are even more people here?"

"Hopefully we will have more introductions by then."

Lady Jane was indeed the more sensible of the two of them. She could be counted on to point out the obvious as well as the sensible in almost any situation. But what would Dosie do without her constant loyalty? "Come, let us sit on that bench by the fountain. Seems a glorious place to be seen at least."

"Yes, and there is shade."

They made their way to the bench and hadn't sat for all of ten seconds when a loud laugh and energetic voice caught their attention. "Mr. Easton?" Dosie's amazed murmur was not lost on Lady Jane.

"Oh no. Not the Eastons." Untitled, all of them, they sat low on Lady Jane's approval list as associations.

But Dosie enjoyed them all. "Now, why not? They are respectable and each one as handsome as the next."

"Yes, and you and Mr. Easton have had enough history to last any season."

"But that's the beauty of him. He is a harmless cohort who might know others and therefore provide introductions."

Lady Jane could not argue that point and so Dosie stood. "Oh, Mr. Easton." She called over to what she could see of his back.

He turned, and his smile grew. His brother at his side smiled ever broader.

Dosie nudged her friend. "Oh look! It's Tauney Easton as well."

Lady Jane smiled and waved. But she groaned beside Dosie.

"Oh come. You know you are pleased."

"Yes, for now, but what if they monopolize our time at the ball?"

"We are not at the ball and have nothing to worry about."

When Julian Easton bowed over her hand, she could only stare for he'd grown twice as handsome, twice as broad and twice as congenial as the last time she'd seen him. "Why Mr. Easton, it has been an age, hasn't it?"

"Indeed it has. You remember my brother, Mr. Tauney Easton?"

"I do. And this is Lady Jane."

"Yes, I remember. Two friends I find together more often than any others, I believe." His smile was charming, and she could feel Lady Jane softening beside her.

After the requisite curtsies and bows, Mr. Julian Easton held his arm out to Dosie. "Care to promenade?"

"Oh yes, we'd like nothing more."

When Lady Jane rested her hand on Mr. Tauney Easton's arm, and they all set out to walk together, they could be nothing but comfortable and at ease as a happy group of four.

"We are grateful to you both as we find ourselves woefully unconnected and in dire need of introductions."

"I'm happy to oblige, though I fear you are far more connected than we."

She could only be pleased with his self-deprecating charm. "Then we shall have to content ourselves with each other."

"So, tell me Lady Theadosia, what are you most looking forward to as we get closer to Christmas and Twelfth Night?"

She smiled. "Well, the Hamilton house party. Will you be going?"

"I have not decided. I've been invited of course. We've been friends with Lord Hamilton since we were lads at Eton. He and Tauney will actually argue over the knot in their cravats." He laughed. "But..."

"But?"

"Edward might push me to do something rash like run away and hide."

"What on earth are you talking about?"

"He's wanting all of us to marry."

She waited and when he said nothing further, she frowned. "That's it?"

"Certainly, that's it. He wants us to marry *now*. And the more time I spend in social situations doing social things, the more I hear about what I should be doing there." He frowned. "Namely finding a wife."

"But it's Christmas. A house party at Christmas time is a lovely event."

"Too true."

"Why are you so opposed to marrying?" The Easton parents had passed, and Dosie knew Edward took his role as eldest brother seriously.

He looked out over the park for a moment and then down into her face. Again, she was stunned at the brightness of his eyes. Had they always been so blue?

"I am not opposed to marrying. I just don't wish to marry on Edward's terms. Goodness, who wants their brother meddling in their affairs."

"Believe me, I understand about meddling in marriage affairs."

"Do you?"

"My father. Just today. Wanted me to consider a courtship I would find loathsome."

"Ho ho! If I promise not to tell this juicy *on dit*, will you share the gentleman's name?"

She looked around, even though no one could possibly be within hearing distance, not even Tauney Easton. "Lord Standish."

"That dark and dreary fellow?"

"Precisely." She shook her head in wonder. "That is exactly what I said to Father."

"Is he moving forward with his demands?"

"No. But I don't believe I've heard the end of it."

He shook his head. "Sounds to me like we're both in quite a pickle."

"Yes, we are." Her burdens seemed heavy all of a sudden. "Can we not simply marry who we choose when we choose?"

"And not be entrapped by the will of another?" He nodded. "I would most certainly hope so."

"Though those words are more simply hoped for coming from a man."

He considered her and she appreciated the sudden light of understanding in his face. "I believe you are correct. Will your father exercise his lawful right to see you married to his choice?"

She started to shake her head. "I don't think so." But she couldn't really be certain. What did she know about how desperate his goals? "I could use some assistance avoiding him at the ball." Her eyes caught his, and he nodded.

"So we understand one another." He patted her hand. "If you ever need a distraction or someone to come save you, I'll do so." He turned a knowing eye in her direction. "If you might do the same for me?"

"Certainly, but what would this involve? What do you mean by needing someone to save me?"

"Oh, nothing too serious, I'm certain. For instance, suppose you are in a group and everyone leaves to dance and you are stuck with Lord Standish. I might show up to catch our dance." He winked.

"That is a remarkable boon. Yes, let's aid one another during this pre-season time in London. There aren't too many in town right now. I imagine we shall always be at the same events." She pressed her fingers into his arm. "But you must come to the Hamiltons'. He will be there."

He studied her a moment, turned back to glance at his brother and then nodded. "We shall attend. Oscar too, no doubt. And Edward." He grimaced.

"What Edward needs is his own wife."

"That's what we all keep saying. One of these days, we're

going to create a joint effort to set the man up. He will have no choice but to marry our pick for his wife."

"I'd love to be there for these antics."

They walked more, talking of nothing and everything and even after the stresses of the morning, Dosie was set quite at ease. So much so that when they had at last finished their promenading, she was laughing with delight. They hadn't met a single other person, but she was pleased.

When the men bowed in front of Lady Jane and herself at her front door, she smiled warmly. "We shall see you at the ball tonight?"

Lady Jane sucked in her breath.

"We shall be delighted to be of service."

"Excellent."

As soon as they had turned the other direction, Lady Jane hissed. "What are you doing?"

"What do you mean?"

"Why are you inviting them to the ball?"

"They were already invited, and don't worry. Mr. Easton and I have an arrangement."

"What kind of arrangement?"

"He's going to help me steer clear of Lord Standish."

She pressed her lips together. "And what if we would like to be with other men at the party?"

"I'm certain the Eastons won't be hovering like lost children. They have their own ladies to woo. This is merely for emergency purposes only."

Chapter Four

As soon as Julian and Tauney walked in the door, Edward called them into his study.

Julian loosened his cravat. "Why do I feel like a lad being summoned by Father?"

"Because Edward views the situation just so."

"Hmm." Julian marched into his father's old study and went straight for the brandy on the sideboard.

"We need to talk." Edward sat in his chair, waving off the brandy Julian offered.

"Come now, this sounds much too serious for the lives we lead." Julian raised his glass and downed it all.

"Sit, brother."

Julian joined Tauney, who had also declined brandy and was sitting with a leg crossed, perfectly relaxed.

"Julian. You need to marry."

He stood back up. "If this is the purpose of the conversation, I think I'll just head back out that door."

"It's time. You are the next eldest and the most adamantly opposed. If you marry, the others will too." Edward stared him down. "Sit. We need to have a conversation."

"Why begin with the most adamantly opposed? I'm certain you could convince Oscar to marry. Just make it a competition." Their other brother competed and won in just about everything he set his mind to.

"You are also my most expensive." Edward lifted a stack of papers from his desk.

"What is this?" Julian sat back down.

"These are all your creditors come calling for their money." He lifted the first paper. "Cards at the Hollisters. You lost the most out of every person there apparently." He lifted the second. "Horse races." Another paper. "Your ridiculous betting at White's." He read from the lists. "Bets regarding Lady Allistair's hair, Mr. Tanning's Cravat, the relationships of half a dozen people...Come, Julian, who bloody cares whether or not Miss Abigail will dance with Lord Panning?"

Julian twisted his neck to loosen his cravat. How had Edward come to know about all that? "It's not as if anyone cares. It was all in fun."

"Except you never win apparently, and have given all your promises for payment." He frowned.

"I can pay them, slowly, with my allowance."

Edward shook his head. "You can pay me."

"What are you talking about?"

"I bought all your debt."

Relief bowled through him. "Oh, excellent. Edward. You are the brother Father knew you would be..."

Edward held up his hand as Julian's voice trailed off. His brother's expression was serious, and Julian sensed there was more coming.

"You owe *me* now. All the debt I paid in your behalf from the races and all over town. I figure it will take your lifetime to earn it back with your commission in the military."

Julian shook his head. *Commission?*

Edward raised his fingers. "Military, church, barrister..."

choose your position. But I can let it go. I'm willing to forgive it all, if you marry."

He stood again. "What!"

"And." Edward held up a finger. "Someone who is not impoverished herself. You must choose your bride by Twelfth Night."

Julian just laughed. "You can't be serious."

"I am more than serious. She must accept your hand by Twelfth Night."

"Or what?"

"Or…you can find your own employment. I've looked up military commissions, Clergy and more schooling to become a barrister. All cheaper than keeping up with your ridiculous bets."

"Edward."

He shook his head. "I am quite serious. Your funds have reached their limit. Marry. Marry well, and all will be forgiven. Or." He cleared his throat and the emotion Julian saw there almost brought out a twinge of sympathy, almost. "Or, you're on your own."

Julian's gut sank and he fell back in his chair. "You're serious?"

"Most dreadfully."

"And the others? You're not cutting them off?"

"They don't cost anything more than their allowances."

"This." Julian stood. He didn't know what else to say. "This is very unbrotherly of you, Edward."

"Look around at the ball tonight. Everyone will be there. Go to some house parties. People have great luck there. Find your bride, convince her to marry you, and all these debts are forgiven."

"And if not? You're serious about the consequences?"

"You can make your own way and pay me back with your own money."

Julian mock bowed. "May our father hear of your selfish use of his money."

"He always said men of honor didn't bet away their money."

Edward's jab stung. Julian knew Father would not be pleased with his recent behavior, even in desperation. "He also said Eastons care for one another."

Edward's face clouded. "I'm doing the best I can with what I know."

And a part of Julian knew Edward truly was doing his best. But he didn't have to like it. And in fact, the more his reality settled in, the angrier he became. He turned on his heels and stomped out of the room. Instead of going upstairs to get ready for the ball, he turned to go outside. Their London townhome sat on a busy street of promenaders. Usually he was pleased to step outside and converse with any number of friends or lovely ladies or make an acquaintance or two. But today he needed to be alone. He wished he were on their estate lands instead. And he wished for his horse. He stepped back inside the house, saying nothing to their butler, Hemstead, and took the stairs going up to his bedchambers two by two.

"Marry indeed." He frowned. There had to be other ways to make money. He dug in his purse. He had money. What did he have left at the bank? Enough? He would head for the tables now. And at the ball. There would be cards at the ball. Get a bunch of men drunk and Julian could earn some. Not enough to pay back Edward, yet. But he had to try.

He summoned his valet and impatiently was dressed for cards. He slipped out the servants' entrance and made his way to one of many disreputable gaming halls.

On the way, he ignored every misgiving that crossed his mind until he stepped inside a smoky, dark building. Men filled the tables. His keen eyes found a good table with men desperate and drunk enough. One held up a hand when he saw Julian approach. "Oh, it's the best of the Easton brothers. Come. Sit." They eagerly added him to their group. That should have been his first clue that the evening would not go well.

Chapter Five

Dosie and Lady Jane stood at the head of the hall, just having entered the large ballroom. People swirled in small groups of excited chatter. "This. Is more than I dreamed." Dosie clasped her hands together. "We must meet everyone and dance every set." She stopped herself from squealing but only just.

"The ball of the year, people are saying. They came into town just to attend. Everyone will be here."

Their dresses complemented each other in such a perfect way. The blue of their ribbons and the gems in their hair were striking. Their matching sapphires shone in the candlelight. Surely they would draw attention and stand out just enough amongst all the other brightly adorned women. And the white of their debutante dresses would alert anyone of their single and hopeful status. She smiled.

"If your father would come, we would have all the introductions in the room that we could ever want." Lady Jane's eyes travelled over the groups to their front.

"I know. I don't know what has him so busy or distracted. It's uncanny. Although, he did say he might come towards the end." Her own mother had been too ill to come. She and

Lady Jane were attending under the care of her friend's aunt. They made their way further into the room. Before she could hide from him, Lord Standish appeared and bowed over her hand. The music began. "I believe we have this set?"

She nodded. "We do, thank you."

"Perhaps I might make an introduction for Lady Jane?"

"Oh, certainly." The man at Lord Standish's side was handsome, tall and friendly, everything he himself was not.

Lady Jane's face lit with surprise.

The two men led them out onto the floor.

"Are you enjoying the ball?" His tone was friendly. Though he hadn't yet smiled, he was perhaps more congenial than she'd ever seen him. Perhaps she would enjoy the set.

"I am. Everyone looks lovely. The ballroom is filling up. This is sure to be the party of the year, don't you think?"

They circled one another, performing the steps, and then stood facing again. "I do as well. I'm pleasantly distracted by all you said, but most especially pleased to see you here."

And he had to make things uncomfortable by being so pointedly focused on a courtship.

She didn't answer but pasted on her small, placid smile and continued the movements in the dance.

"I apologize if I make you uncomfortable. It is only once in a man's life he finds someone so perfectly suited to his tastes. I shall attempt to keep my raptures to myself, for now."

She nodded, not at all certain what she was meant to say to respond to a comment like his. Thank you? I'm sorry I cannot return your rapture? She kept back a frustrated sigh, but only just. The benefit of the set turned out to be the other gentlemen she danced with as they made their way down the line. All showed a genuine interest, and all provided an intro-duction. She grinned. Hopefully her dances would all be filled with pleased and smiling gentlemen.

As soon as the dance ended, she took steps to find Lady Jane, but another gentleman approached. He nodded at Lord

Standish, who stood at her side, and offered his arm. "Might I have this set?"

"Certainly."

She had just met him in the line. "Lord Grandin. You are a marvelous dancer."

"And I enjoyed your dancing as well." They stepped closer, bowed and curtsied, and then began again. This set was more of a reel and fast paced, and long.

She smiled, thinking of all the time apart from Lord Standish. He hadn't asked another to dance, and watched from the side as though serving as her chaperone.

"Does Lord Standish hold a particular interest?" Lord Grandin eyed him over her shoulder.

"Oh, who can say? I have only just met him."

He nodded. "I can understand why a man would linger closer after a set with you." His smile was genuine and his flirting fun.

"Oh you are too complimentary. I think I shall blush." The smile up into his face was encouraging, or at least she hoped it to be. She really had no idea what she was doing, she realized. Every attempt felt more awkward than clever.

Toward the end of their set she became aware of a rustle throughout the room, a hushed whispered gossip.

"Did you hear that?"

"Hear what?" Lord Grandin followed her gaze.

People were fanning themselves and talking and pointing toward the front of the room.

"Oh."

Mr. Julian Easton swayed in place as he stood at the entrance of the ballroom. He was disheveled enough and uncaring enough that Dosie thought him in his cups.

"Someone needs to take Easton out to the gardens to walk off whatever he's come from." Lord Grandin shook his head.

What could have come over him to present himself here in such a state? And how could he serve as her rescuer from Lord

Standish if he was not even aware of his surroundings, which he seemed to not be.

"Good family, the Eastons. And Julian Easton one of the best. He must be really struggling to appear thus. Who can know?" He led her straight down the middle of their line for the last few bars of the dance. Then he bowed. "Thank you. I enjoyed our dance. Perhaps you might save me another set?"

"Certainly." She curtsied, and he brought her to the lemonade tables. She took out her fan to attempt to cool her face.

"I'm always parched after a reel." The fingers that held her cup brushed hers as he handed it over.

They were flirting! She smiled and lowered her lashes. "You have brought me exactly what I most desired. Thank you."

Lady Jane and her dance partner approached. Introductions were made and the couples promptly switched for the next set.

The evening continued with one partner showing up after another so that neither Dosie nor Lady Jane were ever without a man to dance with. But through it all, Dosie kept her eye on Mr. Easton. They had agreed to be of assistance to each other, and they were friends. He was obviously struggling. Unsure what she could do, she knew she must try. As soon as she could, she found a moment to excuse herself on the pretense of a visit to the ladies' receiving room and went to intercept him.

Chapter Six

Hours earlier, bleary eyed, with too many drinks in him, Julian had left the gaming hall, a total failure, owing more than Edward would believe. With each loss he attempted to win more and downed his despair in drink. He staggered a bit in the street. He had to go to the ball. They had tables. Cards. Money changed hands. He would win back what he just lost at least, come out even. Edward wouldn't have to know. He fisted his hands. Curse Edward. Why was he afraid to be brought to task by a brother? Father was gone. They had no manager of their lives. He waved down a hack, jumped in, and gave directions to the ball without thinking.

He tried to walk upright as he made his way to the hosts, bowing, kissing gloved hands and passing by, hardly knowing what he said. He may have danced a set, partially aware. He dropped to a chair for a moment to collect his thoughts. The far door had cards. They must. He stood again. He tried to skirt the edges of the ball, not seeing any faces, to make it to the tables as quickly as possible. He had no coin. They'd let him in on credit, surely. He almost stumbled but corrected and laughed at his clumsiness to whomever was near.

Then someone stood in his way. A woman. She smelled nice.

"Mr. Easton."

"Oh, excuse me." He stepped aside, making his way toward the cards, but she tugged his arm.

He turned, and Lady Theadosia's shocked face looked up into his own. "You are drunk." She hissed.

"Don't tell." He grinned.

"I'm afraid it's painfully obvious." She looked him over. "And you're a sight." She looked around. "Let's get you out into a hall."

"I'll be fine. I'm just heading to cards. They don't care what a chap looks like in there."

"They most certainly do."

He shook his head and then paused. Perhaps they did? He couldn't remember now what they cared about at a ball. They certainly didn't care at the hell where he'd just been. He squinted. "I don't feel well."

"Oh dear." She tugged at his sleeve. They made their way almost to the door but then he lunged for the nearest plant and lost the contents of his stomach inside.

"Dreadful." She dangled a handkerchief over his shoulder in his face. It smelled of lemons and helped calm his stomach. "Thank you."

After wiping his face and mouth, he pocketed her gift and stood, brushing off his jacket. "And now, if you'll excuse me?" He bowed, mostly steady, and turned to leave to find the card room.

"Mr. Easton."

Something about her tone made him pause.

She stood with hands on her hips, an accusing stare on her face.

"Your ladyship?" He waited.

"You promised to assist me this evening."

Had he? Parts of their walk in the park came back to him. Oh, he had. But that was just in fun, mostly. It wasn't as if he was babysitting the chit through every social event.

"So I did. I shall be available to do my duties after I attend to important business."

She huffed and turned from him, but he had no time to care for the sensibilities of his friend. She would get over it soon enough. As soon as the next gossip rolled through the room, she'd be well and truly distracted. Wouldn't she? Perhaps she wasn't quite like that. He shook his head. Time to think of saving his hide.

The tables were full. *Blast!* He stood behind the most likely group and watched each man, each face. He eyed their cards until they looked over their shoulders at him. He backed away. "Just waiting my turn."

But no one seemed ready to give up their spot. And as the cups lifted and the drinks flowed freely, he watched others grow rich as he most desperately looked on. As the evening grew later, he began to give up. But a Lord Potts stood. "You can have my spot, Easton."

Julian leapt for his seat. But when he saw who he shared the table with, he groaned inside. Each wealthier than the last, each shrewd. Each with a large stack of coins in front of them. And each someone Julian had owed money to in the past.

Lord Potts called over his shoulder. "Make sure he has the blunt to begin."

Julian shook his head. "Now, gentlemen. I didn't bring much to the ball, naturally. I'm sure my credit is good with you?" He held his hands out, trying for his most charming smile.

One by one, they shook their heads. "If you don't have any to start, you're out."

He tried to talk his way into the game, but they were

adamant. And then another lord he'd seen at the gaming hall earlier called out across the room. "Don't let him in. They cleaned him out at Higgins' this afternoon."

Julian looked around the room. Perhaps it was the drink wearing off or the reality of his life settling in, but the disgust on some of their faces, the pity on others, the overall disdain was more than he could bear. He stood and left without another word. Entering the ballroom seemed to be more than he could handle at the moment as well. He stood on the very outside edge, watching the smiling-faced guests dance a reel. A group of women walked by, turning, with ready smiles that turned to disdain and whispered conversation, obviously about him. Grateful for the shadows, he considered his sorry state. He was broke, beyond broke. When Edward found out his new debts, lost in one afternoon of cards, he would be livid. With his current state and unkempt display at the ball, Julian might have just lost his opportunity even to marry and be rid of it all. Instead he might be bound for a military commission and a lifetime to pay off his debts. He might *never* marry. The thought opened up a lifetime of loneliness. He thought of his sister Tabitha and her two boys. He loved the lads. Henry, one of his best friends, had married his sister and since then, he knew that one day, one day he would have a marriage like theirs. Had he just lost his opportunity? If it came to a military commission, what respectable woman would want to marry a penniless solider? And if he had a commission right now, he couldn't marry a single one of these women. Who would want to *wait* for a penniless soldier? And further, what person would give a clergy position to a reprobate drunken gambler?

As the reality of his new life settled upon him, he began to take an accounting of the lowness of his behavior and his treatment of Edward. His shoulders drooped. And his ridiculous gambling. There were more ways and better ways to make a living.

And now he must convince one of these lovely ladies to marry him? As he looked from lady to lady, he shook his head. Again, who would want to marry him? Here he was, barely presentable for a ball, throwing up in front of Lady Theadosia, trying to gamble away money he didn't have. He stared at his hessians. Drops of vomit were encrusted near his toes. Who, indeed.

He skirted the edge of the ballroom ready to leave. Movement caught his eye, and the rustle of skirts out a door.

He almost ignored the couple obviously on their way to find a quiet place until he heard a muffled sound, and it was just odd enough that he dragged his feet in that direction to be certain.

The couple moved around another corner, but this time he was almost certain he saw Lady Theadosia's skirts. They were headed for the balcony, the verandah that was visible to all in the ballroom, and she did not seem happy. He picked up his pace.

"You will unhand me at once!" Lady Theadosia's voice sounded courageous. Julian was proud of her. But he picked up his feet to a run.

As he turned the corner, the sound of material tearing made him shout. "Unhand her at once." He dashed out onto the verandah just as Lord Standish pulled Lady Theadosia in an obviously unwanted embrace, visible to any who would care to see through the windows. He wrenched her resisting body closer and pressed his lips to hers in a firmness that was sure to bruise.

Julian ran to him, pulled his surprisingly strong body away and sent a fist to his face. Standish staggered back, one hand at his jaw, his eyes flaming in anger.

Julian scooted Lady Theadosia behind him and stood taller, ready to do whatever it took. "Stand down, Lord Standish. This lady wants nothing to do with you."

He sneered. "Says you. I say she just accepted my proposal of marriage."

"He's lying!" Lady Theadosia's voice shook behind him.

"Her dress is torn." Someone from the crowd that had now gathered called out. And then the Earl of Hunting, Lady Theadosia's father, walked out to join them. "What is the meaning of this!"

Lord Standish bowed. "I have proposed, and your daughter has accepted my hand in marriage. In a moment of celebration, I fear my kisses became too passionate. But since we are to be married, it is only to be celebrated at this point, no?"

Her father looked resigned, almost manipulated, which Julian found unsettling. He stood closer to Lady Theadosia, who was now trembling beside him. "I came upon him forcing himself upon your daughter. There was no acceptance, no agreement in what I could see."

"I did not accept Lord Standish's hand. Listen to Mr. Easton, Father. He-He saved me."

Her father's eyes were disturbed, guilty even, as he stepped closer but kept his voice raised. "But, daughter, you are ruined now. See your dress. Everyone in the ton has seen the incident. Perhaps a marriage to this nice lord will solve everything."

"No." Her strangled whisper was more than Julian could take at the moment. He tried to make his voice sound clear and sure even though his heart shook his chest with newfound courage. "I will marry her."

Several women in the room gasped.

"It could have been me as well as Lord Standish. We were both here together with her. Who's to say? I will do my duty and marry her."

"What are you doing?" Her whispers in his ear gave him greater strength.

"Play along. Surely we can fix this quietly."

She cleared her throat and clung to his sleeve. "Yes, Father. If I must marry, he is the one I choose."

Julian put his arm around her. She stiffened but at least she allowed him to keep her close. It helped with appearances. They could handle this very public display properly and then take care of everything in her father's study after. Surely he wouldn't keep her bound to such a ridiculous attempt to entrap her. But even if he did, Julian was willing to do his duty by her. His friend trembled. He worried her legs would give out altogether.

Lord Standish looked as though he would lose his temper any second. Julian didn't know a face could turn so red.

"Perhaps you and Lord Standish should come to my home tomorrow morning together. We will discuss the particulars."

Julian bowed. "With pleasure." He helped Lady Theadosia keep her dress together and brought her to her father. "In the meantime, perhaps, a carriage?"

"Oh certainly." The man looked as though he'd just awoken to the embarrassment everything surely caused his daughter. He put his arm around her.

Lady Jane ran in at this moment, her eyes growing almost wider than her face. She hurried to Lady Theodosia, and the two of them exited as quickly as possible.

As the crowds began to clear, Lord Standish stepped closer, his foul breath melting Julian's face. "You will regret this. You don't even know what you've found yourself entangled with."

"I am quite certain you are correct. On both counts. But under the circumstances, I didn't see another course of action. I'll see you tomorrow." He turned on his heels and made his way to the door. Instead of waiting for the Easton carriage, he stepped out into the night air and started to make his way home by foot. At least at this point, his steps were steady and his gait straight. He'd lost the last of the influence of drink at last.

And what had he gained?

A confounded mess.

The memory of Lady Theadosia's full and grateful eyes stayed with him. At least he'd done some measure of good that day. Or had he? In all his disrepute, he, Julian, had to be a better option than Lord Standish, didn't he?

Chapter Seven

osie's very center was trembling. She couldn't get herself to calm. The carriage moved through town, and she shook, Lady Jane's arms around her. Her father sat on the other side of the equipage and he wouldn't look at her.

"Father, say something."

"I never thought I'd be in this situation."

"What are you talking about?"

"A daughter, shamed and ruined in front of the ton."

"You-You act as though this is my fault. Father, he dragged me from the room, he forcefully pushed me out to where people could see, ripped my dress and forced a kiss upon me. Surely." She shivered. "Surely you can see how I've been attacked."

He didn't answer.

"Father, answer me."

He looked away.

When Lady Jane exited the carriage, Dosie immediately missed her reassurances. "Is Mother well?"

"You mustn't upset her with this news."

"But I need to talk to her. She will see. She will understand. You're not being reasonable."

"Who's not being reasonable? You wanted to choose your own husband. And now you are forced to marry. Who is not being reasonable?"

"Are you hearing what I'm saying? Lord Standish did this."

"Let us meet in my office." His eyes went to the servants, her maid, the footman outside the carriage.

She sighed.

Once they were inside the home and situated in his study with the door closed, he sat. She remained standing.

"This will not come as happy news. But tomorrow when the two men show up, I will choose Lord Standish as your husband."

She sunk into the nearest chair, feeling the life drain from her face, her arms, her feet. Everything tingled. "No, Father."

"He came to me earlier this month with a proposition, an arrangement that I agreed to. Without consulting you, I thought him a good enough match."

"Father."

"It is done. Some agreements you cannot back out of, not without repercussions. And he's a far better match than Mr. Easton. That man hasn't a penny to his name. Nor title."

"But you saw Mr. Easton. Lord Standish's plan backfired. You surely cannot account for your own daughter's refusal? If you tell him I refuse, what can he do?"

"He can and has insisted that I enforce my role as your father. The law is on my side. I simply sign the papers and you will marry him."

"And if I leave? If I refuse to open my mouth at the wedding? If I refuse to dress, to move? Will you carry me in on a stretcher?"

"Do not make this ridiculous."

"It is already ridiculous, Father. What has happened? What have you done that puts us in this bind?"

His face crumpled and then he rested his forehead in his hands.

Dosie clutched her dress at her heart, lowering herself into a chair, everything inside tightening in pain. "Father?"

"It has been done. There's nothing more I can do."

She watched him in silence. He said nothing more for many moments. And then she slowly rose from her chair and walked out of the room, numb in panic.

The more she walked, the faster her feet picked up. What if Mr. Easton did not come? He'd been drunk. What if he didn't even remember? What if he changed his mind? He was her only hope.

And why would he want to become entangled in her life?

She choked. Mr. Easton was the best she could hope for? Just yesterday her marriage prospects had been open to anyone, and now it was limited to two. One really.

She rushed into her room. "We must pack."

"What?" Her maid Lucy's mouth dropped open.

"You heard me. Pack the necessities. I don't know if we will need them, but we very well could. Pack your own as well."

"But, my lady, where are we going?"

"We might need to run."

Her mouth dropped fully and a stubborn set to her mouth told Dosie she needed to explain some things. She sat down. "Sit." She patted her bed.

"I couldn't."

"It's all right. Sit. I need to tell you what just happened."

She nodded, hesitantly, and then sat so rigidly, with so much discomfort that Dosie waved her hand. "Oh, stand if you must."

She stood immediately.

"I was imposed upon at the ball tonight." She showed her the ripped dress under her cloak.

The gasp told Dosie the girl at least understood the possible implications.

"Lord Standish tried to force himself upon me in a public way, to ensure our marriage."

"No!" Her hands went to the sides of her face.

"Yes. But then a Mr. Easton stepped in to defend me."

"Oh!" Her girlish delight at such a thing would have been amusing in any other circumstance.

"Yes. And he punched Lord Standish. But Father came in. And both men offered for my hand."

"My, this is exciting."

"But Father is trying to force me to accept Lord Standish who is abhorrent, and what if Mr. Easton backs away? What if Lord Standish reaches him too? And makes some kind of threat or...or bargain?" She gasped, thinking of it. "I must write Mr. Easton a note right now." She rushed to her writing table. "But the short of it is, I will not marry Lord Standish. And if Father tries to force me, I will run."

"But where will you go?"

"We will go to our estate, of course. And then from there, I don't know. I will consult Mama."

Father had said she was too ill to deal with these matters, but surely she would want to know if her daughter was running away.

Chapter Eight

J ulian made his way home from the ball slowly, as slowly as possible, dreading every moment of Edward's discovery of his behavior. Though, the brother would have to be pleased about one thing. He snorted. Julian was to be married.

He ran a hand through his hair more than ten times, and he still couldn't make sense of what happened. He was to be married. Was he to be married? No amount of fussing his hair could change the fact that he had very publicly claimed Lady Theadosia as his intended.

A man could do worse. He chided himself. She would do worse. He was the worse. She was one of the most sought-after new debutantes. She had a title, a substantial dowry, a lovely family. She was impeccable in every way, and now she was stuck with him, a gambling reprobate who showed up to balls in his cups desperate for some blunt. He walked for many minutes and found himself in front of Lady Theadosia's town-home. He lowered himself onto the ground, leaning back against a tree, and stared up into the darkness of the home.

Lights flickered inside as people were likely attending to the evening duties and making their way into bed. What was

Lady Theadosia thinking up there? Likely devastated. No woman wanted to begin her first Season in London with scandal and a forced marriage. She'd avoided Lord Standish but landed with Julian as a husband. And considering his state, he didn't wish himself on any woman.

Hours passed. His body grew chilled. His legs numb. But he sat at the tree anyway. Voices shook him from his stupor. Men passing, paused in front of the home across the street. "She will be mine, gentleman. That Easton fellow won't even show up tomorrow. Her father prefers me." He laughed. "Who wouldn't?"

Standish.

The sounds of coin passing hands tinkled in his ears. Julian frowned. They didn't think him reliable enough to show up and meet his commitments? Her father preferred that snake of a man to him? His head fell into his hands. What would his own father say of his behavior? Up until protecting Lady Theadosia, Julian hadn't done too much that would please his father. But he knew that he'd done well by the lady. He'd done what any Easton should do, any honorable man, and he, Julian, was raised to be an honorable man.

As the men moved past and away down the street, he stood, talking to himself. "It's time, Julian. It's time for you to be an Easton."

Chapter Nine

"I don't know if your mother will be much help to you now. She is needing *you*. Or someone. She's ill."

Dosie's alarm grew as she tried to make sense of her maid's words. "My mother is ill?"

"Oh, she is ill indeed."

"What? What do you know?"

"She sent servants away this afternoon, just wanted to be alone. She has the fevers now."

"Oh no!" She dropped the writing materials at her desk and ran from the room. Her feet took her down the hall. A footman stood in front of her mother's door, but she hardly stopped. "Stand aside."

He did and she rushed into the room. It stank of something awful. She ran to the windows, opening the curtains wide to let in some moonlight. She lit a candle and carried it closer to the bed.

The covers were piled high. In the darkness, she could hardly see a sleeping form. "Mama?"

For a moment no one responded. She stepped closer, peering into the darkness, commanding her eyes to adjust to the light. "Where are you? Can you hear me? Mama?"

Movement in the bed brought sighs of relief. "Oh, thank heavens. Mama." She moved to the side, reaching out to touch what looked like her head.

She burned with heat.

Dosie pulled back the covers. "She is hot to the touch. Someone!"

Her mother's maid popped into the room.

"Has the doctor been called?"

She bobbed a curtsey. "No ma'am."

"What! Heavens. Call for the doctor. Get a footman in here."

"Yes, my lady."

The footman stepped in the door, seeming ready for just such a summons.

"Get the doctor."

"Yes, my lady." He ran as though he knew the urgency. What was wrong with everyone? Why hadn't the doctor already been called? "Dorcas."

"Yes, my lady."

"Call for Cook."

She ran from the room.

Dosie hurried to her mother's water pitcher. It was dry. Aghast, she rang the bell. As soon as someone came, she handed them the pitcher. "Bring me water and lots of rags. Hurry. Run!"

They ran from the room.

She felt a presence behind her. Her maid. "Lucy, thank you for letting me know."

"Beggin' your pardon, my lady. Your father needn't know."

She turned to her. "What are you saying?"

"I'm not saying anything except he needn't know that I was the one who told you."

She studied her maid and the implications sank deep inside. Things were much worse than she imagined.

They returned with the water. Cook arrived in a bustle. "I've brought my powders. They're bringing up a tea tray. Heavens above!" she exclaimed when she saw Dosie's mother. "We need to get this woman out of her clothes and into new ones."

Dosie let them get to work. She stood back, wringing her hands. How had things gotten to this point?

After what felt like half the night, her mother had new bedclothes, new bedding and a fresh wet, cool cloth on her forehead consistently.

At last the doctor arrived.

"Oh, Dr. Jones, thank you." She rushed to him.

"How long has she been thus?"

Dosie looked to Dorcas.

She dipped her head. "Two days."

"Get that woman something to drink." He hurried to her side.

"Cook has her powders."

He waved them away. Then he turned. "Mrs. Smiths' powders work miracles. But now she needs water most of all."

Dosie paced at the back of the room, growing more and more anxious. How could this have happened? What exactly had happened? Had her father simply left his wife to die? Surely not. But Dosie could see no other explanation. Her mother still responded to no one.

Dosie clenched her fists. The portrait of her parents above the mantel, smiling at each other, mocked their current situation so that she wanted to tear it from the wall. The bough of holly her mother always placed above her mantle seemed a mockery of Christmas hope.

"She's drinking," the doctor called in a soft voice.

"Oh thank heavens." She clutched her hands together at her front.

"And she's not nearly as hot," Dorcas called over to Dosie. She glanced up at the doctor. "Beggin' your pardon."

"No, speak up, woman. We need all our help." He turned to Cook. "Have you your powders for fever?"

"Yes, with me right here." She handed them over.

"Very good." He sniffed them. "Excellent. This will work well. Steep and give her as much as she will take as often as she will take it. My guess is at first it will be few sips far and between. But the more the better. And of course, keep trying to get her to drink water."

Dosie fell back into a chair in the corner.

The doctor turned to her. "I think she will be all right. Be we stepped in just in time." He shook his head as if he couldn't believe things had gotten to this state. Neither could Dosie.

"Will she be well enough to travel?"

"When she can sit up and take food, she could travel carefully in a coach if kept warm enough. You considering your estate property?"

"Yes, I think it might be wise to travel there."

He nodded. Their shared expression spoke things she didn't dare put into words. As soon as he left, she pulled aside Lucy. "Don't forget. Pack our bags."

She nodded and hurried from the room.

Chapter Ten

J ulian paced the floor in his room. He'd dismissed his valet hours ago. Sleep would not come. He repeated again and again the same thoughts, the same questions, the same condemnation, the same call to betterment. Be an Easton. Be a bloody Easton. Was he to be married then? To Lady Theadosia? He shook his head. She was a perfectly fine woman. He enjoyed her attention. Made a point of dancing with her when possible. They'd come up with this crazy idea to help one another. But…never had he considered marriage. Marriage. And he cringed at the thought. And to Lady Theadosia, someone who had seen him at his worst. He hated that she saw him as a drunken wastrel. He hated that he must have lost her respect. If he would enter into a marriage with a woman, he would want to offer something, to provide for her, to bring something to the marriage of value. As it was, he brought only debt. And shame. How had he fallen so low?

He fell onto his bed, wishing to fall into the depths of darkness and forget that today happened. But shortly after he closed his eyes, his door banged open.

Julian lifted his head.

Edward stood in the doorway in his nightclothes with a candle in his hand.

"Brother." He moaned.

"What have you done?"

"Well, you'll be happy to know I'm getting married."

"Did you wrack up as much debt as possible as a punishment before you at last did your duty?"

"No, brother."

"What are these notes from creditors that keep arriving?"

"I was trying to earn some money, make up for all the debt." His head fell back on his bed. "And I went about it the wrong way. I got drunk. I was desperate."

Edward didn't say anything, but Julian felt his presence like he would have his own father's. Perhaps the man stood next to his eldest like a ghost, trying to impress upon Julian his own waste of a life.

"I know. You don't even have to say what a mess I am. And now a woman I admire has agreed to marry me, but I'm coming at this all wrong. I'm at my lowest low. What have I to offer her? No woman wants to be strapped to me."

Edward moved closer and sat on Julian's bed. "Tell me what happened. I've heard all kinds of things already."

"In the middle of the night?"

"Yes, some of it came with the claims for debts to be paid. Maybe they think you'll have some money now that you're getting married."

Julian groaned again.

"What is bothering you most?"

He rolled over and stared at the ceiling. "That I have sunk so low. I daren't look my new wife in the face."

"But from what people say, you are saving her from ruin. I think that has to count for something. I'd say you're even."

He sat up, a new hope alighting. Then he told Edward the lot of it. His sorry evening came out in full humiliation, but as he got to the part of his rescue of Lady Theadosia, he couldn't help but have a bit of hope. "Do you know, you're right? Perhaps I have made amends for some of what I lack."

"Of course. That's the spirit. Go rescue your fair maiden so she can save your sorry self from ruin and we can all feel better in the morning."

Julian laughed, a low kind of humorless laugh. "May your marriage begin on more hopeful terms."

"One can only hope I will be so blessed." The wistful sound of Edward's voice was not lost on Julian. Was his brother waiting to marry off all the brothers before he himself got married? "You take Father's wishes too much to heart. He would want you happy as well as all of us."

"I know." Edward stood. "Get some sleep. From what I hear, Lord Standish is not going to let this go lightly, and her father may have reason to support him over you."

"What do you know?"

Edward shook his head. "That's all I know. Something's amiss there."

A footman arrived in his doorway. "Beggin' your pardon. We've just received a message from the Manet household."

Edward took the paper and handed it to Julian, joining him with the candlelight.

"It's from Lady Theadosia." He broke the seal and unfolded the parchment.

Dear Mr. Easton,

Things are more amiss than you likely realize. You have well and truly saved me. I know you perhaps hoped to clear things up in my father's study tomorrow, perhaps avoid marriage altogether, but unless we marry, I will be well and truly attached to the loathsome Lord Standish. I beg you to please hold true to your promises made in front of so many and marry me as you said. Even though I will likely not be in the meeting, know I am with you, heart and soul and cheering for your success. I feel my every happiness relies upon this success. And thank you. In whatever ways I can, for the rest of our lives, I will live in gratitude.

Hopefully yours,

Lady Theadosia

"There. See? You have rescued her."

He frowned. What could be amiss? Who was this Lord Standish and what was he entangled in? "But it won't be easy. Shall I bring my solicitor? And a barrister perhaps?"

"And perhaps I should come as well, another witness from the gentry?"

"Yes, thank you." He sat. "Shall I write her? Solidify my plans? Leave evidence of my wishes?"

"Certainly." Edward stood. He paused, took a step, opened his mouth and then closed it again.

"What is it? Speak up, brother."

"I regret saying this. I should keep myself well and truly quiet."

"Out with it, man."

"You don't have to do this."

"What?"

"He said he'd marry her. She is saved by another."

"But you heard her. She hates him. He might be cruel. He is not the good sort of man."

Edward breathed out in relief. "Then you are moving of your own accord."

"Yes, I feel I must, as a gentleman." He placed a hand on Edward's sleeve. "Though it does encourage me that you have a heart after all, that you would ensure I am moving forward of my own volition."

"Yes, I have a heart."

Julian stopped and pulled Edward into an embrace. "You do, brother. I know it. Thank you."

"You're welcome. I don't know what you're thanking me for, but hopefully this will be good for you. She's got plenty of money and estates besides."

"And she's a good enough sort of person. We get along well." Julian smiled. And then nodded. "Yes, I think we can move forward quite happily."

He took out his quill, dipped it in ink and began to write. Edward left him to it with promises to summon the solicitor and barrister.

When he had finished and was satisfied with his words, he sealed the letter and sent it back to Lady Theadosia's townhome. Then he leaned back in his chair, stretched his arms and, for the first time all day, felt a semblance of peace. "Now to bed with me so that I'm not bleary eyed when I arrive at the man's study in the morning." He looked around at the silence in his room. Yes, he was talking to himself. But yes, he didn't think quite so lowly of himself as he had just hours before. Perhaps he was doing a bit of good for another in just a few hours.

With those thoughts, he drifted off to sleep if not with a smile, at least with some contentment.

But he awoke with the headache of the ages. And his mood was foul, his face, a tired disaster, his patience at an all-time low, but his determination strong.

His solicitor and barrister had both agreed to come and Edward along with them. They all knocked on Lord Hunting's door together.

He opened and was taken aback a moment before allowing them to enter. "Gentlemen." He dipped his head. Despite his questionable reaction, the man had significant influence and had to this point, seemed an honorable person.

Julian stepped in last and held out his hand. "Lord Hunting. I'm pleased to be able to finalize things with you. But I wish to do this the correct way. Might I have a moment to properly ask for your daughter's hand?"

"Oh, that won't be necessary. I think once we have a conversation, you will see that you are well and truly free of your obligations here and may carry on as you were."

"Oh, no. With respect, we are here to show otherwise."

He frowned. "You would argue for her hand?

"I will, my lord. Perhaps in gratitude for the time she

rescued me as children?" His attempt to bring to remembrance the closeness of their families, to bring jest to a singularly tense conversation fell on deaf ears. With no responding smile from Theadosia's father, Julian continued, "We have been friends for a good time now and had come to an agreement earlier in the day."

"Earlier in the day?"

He nodded. "Yes. We happened upon one another in the park and she asked me especially to be aware and come to her rescue for just such an event to take place." It wasn't quite what she had predicted would happen, but the intent had been the same. He was certain of it.

He turned to the barrister. "And I have the others here to expedite the process of communicating all negotiations."

"I see. Well, do come in." He led them into his study where Lord Standish was already waiting. He stood. "Come to clear up your gambling debts are you, Mr. Easton?"

"Gambling debts?" Lord Hunting's frown deepened, his sharp eyes turning to Julian.

Julian bristled and then his shoulders lowered in shameful admittance of his sorry state, but Edward placed a hand on his back. "I've actually already taken care of his debts. We've come to wish a new couple every happiness."

Chapter Eleven

osie peered out her window down to the street at the group of men Mr. Easton had brought with him. Her heart beat with happiness. He had come. Her mother was doing much better. She was taking fluid regularly. Her color was back. The doctor said she would be well. And now Mr. Easton had come to fight for her hand. She smiled. And took out his letter again to re-read.

Dear Lady Theadosia,

Have no fear I will renege on my promises. I am a man of my word. I appreciate your warning. We will come prepared for anything. Once papers have been signed and all decided, what say you of a special license? We can discuss the particulars when I propose as you deserve to hear it said. But for now, have no fear, dear friend. I will be there.

Yours truly,

Mr. Easton

"He is a good man, is he not?"

Lucy didn't answer, just nodded while she hummed away, cleaning the room.

Dosie left to check on her mother. She'd not seen a bit of her father since their meeting in his study. He'd not visited her mother. He'd not been upstairs as far as she could tell. Something was gravely amiss. The sooner she and her mother left London the better. She stepped quietly, not wishing to wake her mother but saw her sitting up, her color much improved, with a book in hand.

"Mother." She stepped forward and held out her hands. "It is so good to see you looking well."

"I am much improved, and I heard from Dorcas that I have you to thank."

"Well, and my own Lucy. I asked about you and she told me you'd taken a turn for the worse." She studied her mother's face. She seemed strong, strong enough to hear some bits of news. "I have news."

"Oh?" She set her book down.

"Mr. Easton is downstairs talking with Father right now."

"Mr. Easton?" Her forehead crinkled. "Oh, the Eastons. Our dear friends?"

"Yes, remember he comes from a family of four brothers and Miss Tabitha who married that nice Lord Courtenay?"

She nodded. "Yes. Of course."

"He has asked me to marry him."

Her mother's eyes lit. "And are you well and truly happy?"

"I am, Mother, the best I can be."

She rested a palm at her daughter's cheek. "Now, what does that mean?"

So, Dosie told her the whole of it and watched her mother's face grow more and more pale. When she was finished, she worried she'd well and truly sent her mother into a relapse. But at last she spoke and Dosie breathed out in relief.

"Your father..." She shook her head. "Well, perhaps it is best left unsaid."

"But Mr. Easton will take care of it. I will marry him and then we need hear from Lord Standish no longer." She put a hand on her arm. "As soon as you are well enough to travel, I think we should return home for the holidays."

She nodded. "Yes."

"Mother." Dosie's heart hurt for what she felt she needed to say to her mother.

She searched her daughter's face. "Your father."

"Yes. He hasn't been up to check on you. He…he hadn't called the doctor." She hated to say these things. She didn't want to hurt or scare her mother.

"He has had a lot on his mind, I'm afraid. Don't be too hard on him. He'll stay here in London with Parliament in session and have much to take care of."

"But you would have died." The words flew out of her mouth, the fear and indignation she'd been keeping inside escaping with them.

But her mother didn't respond in any way Dosie thought merited the circumstance. She kept avoiding the issue and pretended there was a good and logical reason.

Dosie didn't know what her mother was talking about, but she hoped it would all be well and that they could be shielded from the worst. "Lord Hamilton is having a house party while we are there. So perhaps we can participate in some of his festivities. Lady Jane is coming."

"Oh, that is excellent. You shall not be without your diversions." Her mother's hand was stronger than she expected as it squeezed hers and her eyes were full of love.

"When do you think you can travel?"

"I will make myself ready to leave tomorrow."

"Are you…quite certain?"

"I believe I can sit or lie in a carriage, yes." She nodded.

Dosie felt great relief. "I will instruct Dorcas to pack."

She nodded. "And now, with that thought to warm me, I think I shall rest."

"Yes, very good." She stepped quietly to her mother's closet where Dorcas had already begun to pack.

"Thank you, Dorcas. We are leaving for the foreseeable future so pack as much as you can, but be quick about it."

"Yes, my lady."

Dosie moved over to the top of the stairwell and began to descend. She didn't know what she expected to see or hear since all conversations were taking place behind a closed door, but she couldn't help feeling drawn to the room, the door that held the news of her new life. How incredibly odd that a few words spoken in there would drastically change everything for her. She hoped and prayed things would be determined according to her best opportunities.

The door to the study opened and before Dosie could run back up the stairs and out of sight, Mr. Easton stepped out into the hall. Immediately his eyes caught sight of her. His smile was firm, and confident and...pitying? No, but compassionate certainly. What had happened inside?

The rest of the men followed him out the door.

Lord Standish stormed past. "You have not heard the last of this." He almost beat the footman to the door, but it was opened and he exited out onto the street without another word.

Her father shook hands with the other men. "Thank you for coming. Thank you for your goodness to my daughter. I'm astounded to find a man such as you in the world, Mr. Easton. To think that you would do this all out of duty and nothing more." He shook his head.

Dosie's heart clenched. Only out of duty? But then she reminded herself that of course Mr. Easton was duty-bound. But now that she'd received all she wished, now that she was free from the clutches of Lord Standish, she had to feel something undefinable about the situation. Guilt? Beholden? She didn't know. But it wasn't altogether pleasant. Certainly she felt gratitude. "Father?"

All eyes turned to her.

"Yes?"

"Might I have a word with Mr. Easton alone?"

"Of course. That seems appropriate, does it not?"

The others shook hands. Edward had come. He nodded to her, his smile warm. While Julian and Edward were still conversing, she approached her father. "Mother is much recovered. Dr. Jones has said we are past the worst."

He started. "Was she that ill?"

"Oh yes, Father, she could have died."

The alarm that grew on his face surprised her. How could a man not know the dealings of his own household? His own wife? "I was told you directly ordered she not be disturbed."

"Well, I did, but that was when she had a headache." He ran a hand through his hair.

"Father, the servants alerted me and when I went to check on her, she was unresponsive. We called the doctor and he has saved her life."

He reached a trembling hand out to the door frame. "You'll excuse me?"

She nodded and watched him race up the stairs. Somewhat relieved, she realized that her father did indeed love her mother.

Mr. Easton approached, studying her face. "What are you thinking?"

She turned to him with her most relieved and happy smile. "That my parents love each other."

He laughed. "And has that come as a surprise?"

"You would not believe the time I've had." She sighed. "Shall we sit?"

"Certainly."

She led him into their front parlor. They each sat on the sofa, close enough to almost touch, but not quite. And then she found herself without words. What to say to the man who had agreed to marry you to save you from an awful situation?

He cleared his throat. "I think the first thing that should happen right now requires me to be down on one knee." He lowered himself to the ground and the sight of him there brought a rush of emotion to her heart. And suddenly her eyes filled with tears. "Oh, I'm sorry."

He rose. "Are you well? Is it that hard to think of? Perhaps you aren't ready for this yet."

"No not at all. In fact, I'm so very ready for this."

He returned to his knee. "You are?"

"Yes. I have had such a time of it and utterly alone. My father, my mother. She almost died."

"What?"

She nodded. "Yes. And I thought my father was at fault. And then worrying about you and that awful Lord Standish. And we are about to travel to our estate to run. Hide." She hiccupped as all this came pouring out of her mouth. And Mr. Easton, bless him, listened as though trying to follow. But how could he honestly?

"And are you still leaving tomorrow?"

"I think so, yes. Come with us?"

He considered her for only one breath. "I will."

She exhaled. "Oh, that is wonderful. I don't know what to say except I am so well and truly happy about the outcome of today's conversation."

He studied her. "Surely you are not enamored with me."

She laughed. "Not at all."

"I wouldn't mind such a thing. It might be nice if some day you and I could." He stopped. "Perhaps I'm getting ahead of myself." He reached for her hand. "Lady Theadosia. Would you do me the honor of becoming my wife?"

She found her eyes filling with tears again. Nodding, she knelt down beside him. "Yes." She placed a hand at the side of his face. "And thank you. I don't know if I'll ever be able to repay you for doing me such a kindness, but I shall spend all my days trying to make our lives wonderful."

He shook his head. "You have done me a great honor and helped me as well. Let us call it even."

They stood and when he pulled her into his arms, she felt

something, surprising perhaps. Something more than friendly about his arms around her, something almost ticklish, but she had no time to analyze things. She'd cried and carried on more than she should already. But she was grateful for one important thing. She no longer had to do life alone. And that felt marvelously magical. When he at last released her, a flash of pleasure in his eyes, she wondered if he too had felt something. "Now, Mr. Easton. Would you care to go for a ride on our estate? And help me tend to the greenhouse?" The more she thought of sharing her home with him, the more pleasant their situation became.

"And might we also find the fishing hole I've heard so much about?"

"Oh certainly, but you will never catch a fish as big as the one I have."

"That is most likely true. A gentleman would never out fish a lady, but I should like to make an attempt." His grin was so boyish, so congenial, she could only smile.

They sat again on the sofa, talking of their memories, the things they shared, and avoiding the difficult situation that had brought them together.

As she thought more about it that night while Lucy combed out her hair, she mused aloud, "Do you think Mr. Easton and I will take breakfast together?"

"Who can say ma'am?"

"And perhaps we'll have a cozy routine, a walk in the evenings, reading books by the fire." She tucked her knees up to her chest. "It will be like having a best friend at my side all the time. Do you suppose he'll enjoy the same games? Does he like Whist?"

Lucy just smiled and braided her hair for bed.

"He's coming with us tomorrow."

"Excellent, my lady."

When she'd at last dismissed Lucy, she thought about her parents. At least they were in love. She smiled. And then for a moment, her lips turned down. Having a friend as a husband was good. But she had always hoped that she would have something more. Perhaps with time. He was a good man, didn't have to marry at all, and yet stepped in to help. She could respect and then learn to love someone like that. Perhaps.

Chapter Twelve

Julian had never prepared for travel faster than he did that evening. Edward had the whole household staff assisting him and before he went to sleep, most of his belongings were packed. Edward joined him as the last of it was being loaded. "I've heard talk that Standish isn't giving up."

"What is wrong with that man? Find a new woman."

"We joke, but he is determined and breathes an unsavory air."

"Yes, I've thought the same. I should marry her, and soon."

"No telling what he will do, but that is wise advice. And perhaps, try to win her over, you know? She's a beautiful, engaging woman. You could be very happy."

"Yes, thank you, brother. I don't offer much, but I shall do my best to encourage her affections. And you, don't be a stranger. It might help my case if she was reminded of all the other more reputable Eastons."

"You could be the best of us for her. I have faith in you, brother." He clasped a hand on Julian's shoulder. "We know where you will be living. We can always visit and bring whatever more you might want from your things."

"Yes, and I'm certain I'll visit the Easton townhome now and again."

"Of course." Edward clapped him on the back. "I'm proud of you, brother."

"Thank you. And I'm sorry I've been such a challenge. Thank you for taking care of all the debt."

"I'm happy things are working out so well."

"Yes, I as well." Things were working out surprisingly well, too easily well. And when that happened, he knew something was about to change.

The carriage arrived at his front stoop early the next morning and the servants made a quick work of storing his trunks. He mounted his horse and approached the side of the carriage. Lady Theadosia's curls filled the window as she peeked out. "Are you sure you won't ride inside with us?"

"Certain. You enjoy your mother and hopefully she can rest and become well." He peered in past Lady Theadosia. "I wish you well, Lady Hunting."

"Thank you, son. It is good to see you again." Her voice sounded weak and he nodded in return, not wishing to engage more of her energies in conversation.

"Thank you." Lady Theadosia's shy smile before she closed the window charmed him and he wished to see it again.

And that was that. The carriage started moving and he rode along beside. This was going to be a long day of travel.

After around five hours, he realized he'd had no idea how long. They would never reach the estate by nightfall. Lady Theadosia's mother was ill, which of course he knew, but he had no idea how such a thing would require them to stop. And for how often. He rode around to the back of the carriage. "You there." He addressed one of the footmen.

"Yes, sir."

"Is there a plan in our travels to sleep at an inn?"

"Yes, in Hampton."

"Ah, thank you." So when they travelled to their estate, they took twice as long as the typical journey would take. Something he wished he'd known heading out. He rode up closer to the window. "Lady Theadosia."

She lifted the curtain and he regretted his interruption immediately. Her mother was not looking well. She lay flat on the seat, her skin pale, her eyes closed. He talked quieter. "How is your mother?"

"She is not as well as we would like. We are considering a stop at a closer inn to give opportunity for more rest."

He nodded. "Is there something I can do?"

Her face warmed to him and the pleasure he saw there made him wish to do something deserving of such a look from her again. Perhaps he could pick flowers along the way? Offer her a ride on his horse? Certainly he was grateful he had curbed his temptation to complain about their slow pace.

"Thank you." She had no task for him to do, but his asking seemed to have done something. She kept the curtain lifted up and they rode along almost companionably for many miles.

After two full days in the saddle and a stay at an uncomfortable inn, they finally turned down the drive to her estate. The entrance sat back behind a fenced green. Trees towered over each side of the drive and the house rose high with pillars along the front. It was immaculately kept. Organized hedgerows, rose gardens, fountains all made up beautiful grounds. Large stretches of green in every direction drew his eyes. Once he'd rested from the saddle, he wanted to ride out over all the land. The closer they drew to the house, the more he realized how magnificent it was. Far larger than their Easton estate, far larger than many he'd been in. Was he to live here? Again, the dark tendrils of doubt and shame crawled up under his skin. What had he to offer this woman, really? He'd brought nothing to the marriage. He provided no wealth, no income, no industry. He brought no title. And up until the day he proposed, he had been on a fast track to becoming a complete gambling reprobate. His breath exhaled, haggard sounding. He was tired. He'd been riding for more than two days. And it was time to take a hot bath.

A line of servants exited the house, their purple and yellow livery standing out magnificently in the sun. Lady Theadosia stepped down from the carriage, greeted them and began what looked like instructions. Eyes glanced in his direction. Servants nodded, and men were summoned from the house with a carrier for her mother.

Lady Theadosia was a wonder—thoughtful, well brought up, organized, and brave.

Servants approached with a mounting block. He waved it off and dismounted. Then he handed the reins to a stable hand. "He likes oats and alfalfa. He needs a good brush and plenty of water."

The lad bowed and led his horse away.

He brushed off his sleeves more out of habit than anything and then approached the house. Their butler bowed. "Mr. Easton."

"Thank you. I'd like to meet you and the staff if I could."

"Certainly. Perhaps you could refresh yourself first as the lady suggested? Baths are being drawn."

"Oh of course. How thoughtful." He dipped his head and followed the footman that was leading the way into the house. And that would be the way of things. The lady of the house and not the master, at least in this case, right now. He was a guest, and an interloper. And he should be all right with that, he told himself as he walked up the stairs. But he didn't completely agree with the assessment.

The rooms he was given were elaborate, spacious, and had the best views. His man directed the placement of the trunks in his closet. Julian walked through his sitting area, passed by his large balcony, and into his closets. His man, Lucio, had a larger room on the other side of the closet. Two doors could close in between them. And on the other side of his room, another door was closed. When he tried it, the latch didn't move. Locked.

A servant entered through a panel.

"What is this?"

"During daylight hours, when you are expecting us, the servants like to use these corridors."

He nodded. "Where are the entrances?"

"You have just the one."

"Excellent."

The servant brought a tray of food and drink and placed it on the table in the sitting room. Then she left through the panel in the wall.

Julian Easton had been raised on a gentleman's estate. His father had sent them to Eton, to Oxford. They had servants, tenants, and lovely living quarters, but Lady Theadosia's upbringing was much grander. And he'd best become accustomed to things, else he seem a simpleton. We couldn't have anyone thinking she married a tenant farmer. "Of course. Of course," he began saying about every new luxury shown him. Until he felt certain the servants were tired of the words.

He ate, bathed, dressed, relaxed, and explored some and still he hadn't seen Lady Theadosia or her mother. They were likely in the family wing of the house which meant he was in a guest room. He supposed that was to be expected. He wondered if he would ever feel like more than a guest in her home.

Chapter Thirteen

❧

He had no right to complain, just the opposite in fact, but he needed something to do.

In his exploring, he stopped a servant. "Might I take a look in the library?"

"Oh certainly. If you would follow me?" The footman seemed very well spoken. He led Julian through a maze of rooms, one adjoining another, until he stopped at a set of double doors. Their thick dark wood appeared inviting as well as formal. The servant opened the doors. Others followed quickly, dusting surfaces, and a maid began to light the fire. Candles were lit, the drapes opened, and Julian walked further into the room. "Thank you for opening up the room. I didn't realize it had been closed to guests."

"Our pleasure sir, certainly. If there is anything else you require?"

"Could I have a tray?"

"Right away."

They left soon after they'd all arrived, and the room was lit and warm and growing more comfortable by the minute.

He wandered up and down five rows of books and then along the outer walls of the room. They had an impressive collection. Certainly he could take up reading more. Perhaps there was something he could do to be gainfully employed. Or of use. He would settle first for of use and then perhaps earning assets would come.

He chose two books he'd like to start: one dealing with shipping to the East Indies, the other, Wellington's battles in the war with Napoleon. They sat on the table, welcoming him, but instead he moved over the windows at the far end of the room, shifted the curtains and looked out over the grounds.

At last he caught a sight of Lady Theadosia, his intended. He smiled and tried to think of her that way. His intended. He repeated the words in his mind until they stuck somewhat. A great feeling of pride rose up inside. His wife. All these years he expected to be stifled by a life of marriage, but now, presented with just such a life, he found it exhilarating, And, as he studied her profile as she looked up into the sun, charming. His intended was a beautiful woman. He'd always thought so. Strange he'd never considered courting her. Why hadn't he? She was everything a man could want in a wife. How blessed to realize such a thing after one proposed. This whole scenario could have played out in multiple ways. And yet, here he was, handed a beautiful life, one he did not deserve.

She turned to him. Perhaps she felt his gaze. The arm she waved was excited, her face smiling large and open.

He waved back, pleased to be the focus of so much of her attention. But then the sound of someone calling to her from above drew his eye. He tried to open his window, but then Lady Theadosia walked closer and continued a conversation with someone above him from the upper floors. She hadn't been waving at him at all.

He turned from the window. His feet suddenly needing to be somewhere, doing something. He rang for a servant.

One appeared immediately. "Yes, Mr. Easton."

"I need something to do."

"Sir?"

"Might I have a task? A tenant needs something, perhaps?" It had been an age since he'd done a single thing for any tenant, but he was desperate to feel needed.

"You might want to consult with Mrs. Hamblin, the housekeeper."

"Excellent. And where might I find her?"

"I'll inform her you require her presence."

"No, I'll go to her, if you would?" He indicated that the servant should lead the way. They walked through the other side of the house that Julian had not yet seen and then skirted the kitchen from which delicious smells made his stomach rumble and then down a hall. "This is her set of offices."

"Thank you." He approached the door and then knocked.

"Come in," an older woman's voice called.

When he peeked in the doorway, she was on her feet in an instant. "Mr. Easton."

"Yes, Mrs. Hamblin. I'm afraid I have startled you. Do forgive me?" He smiled his most charming smile until she returned the expression.

"I was wondering. Could you direct me to the tenants?"

"The tenants, sir?"

"Yes, I wish to be of use and I'm certain there is something to be done for the tenants."

She considered him for one long moment and then a spark of admiration lit her eyes. "I do believe you are serious."

"Yes, quite."

"Well then, yes. It has been many months since a man of the house has engaged himself in caring for the tenants. Every time we hear of a request for help, I write it in a ledger." She lifted a black, leather bound book.

"And is that the ledger?"

"The very one."

When it was placed in his hand, he ran fingers over the soft leather and then opened it. "This is excellent, thank you."

He nodded, running his finger down the lines. "And might I have a few footmen to assist me?"

"You might. I shall summon them, and they will meet you outside the front door in thirty minutes?"

"Excellent; you have anticipated my very request. That would be perfect."

Soon he had a donkey cart and a team of three footmen. Their cart had items to patch roofs, to fix fences, to dig about in the dirt. He wondered just what all the tenants needed, but he was given a list and the addresses and instructions.

They made their way to the first home, and his heart felt somewhat comforted. Assist the tenants. He could do that. He could be of use in this way. And he didn't feel like he was just waiting for her to send some attention his way.

Chapter Fourteen

✦

osie at last felt like things were in order at her home. Her mother was situated. The servants were made aware of the plans—her and Mr. Easton's upcoming nuptials as well as their intended stay. There were so many questions she hadn't been expecting. And then she'd wanted to see everyone, kiss Cook on the cheek, say hello to Thomas, their gardener. She wrote a note to Lady Jane, explaining everything. But at last, she felt well and truly moved back in to her home and she went in search of Mr. Easton.

But no one as yet knew where he was. Some had seen him in the library. Dosie was glad. She was rather proud of her parents' collections. She poked and prodded and searched almost every room with still no sign of him until Mrs. Hamblin happened upon her.

"Oh, Mrs. Hamblin. Do you know where Mr. Easton has gone?"

She surprised Dosie by putting her hand at her chest in a most exuberant manner. "Oh, my lady. You've found a good one in that Mr. Easton."

"Yes. Thank you." She smiled politely, wondering what had come over their typically staid and practical housekeeper.

"He has requested a list of the tenants and all their needs and has set out with some servants and a donkey cart."

She was astounded at the news. "Do you know which direction they have gone?"

"I certainly do. But they left over an hour ago, so they could be anywhere by now, but their first stop was the Hendersons'."

"Thank you." She turned. "I think I should like to go for a ride. Ready my horse." She climbed the stairs while a footman ran out to deliver the message to the stables.

Lucy soon had her in riding habit and the horse was out in front. "Let's see what is afoot, shall we?" She spoke to no one in particular and no one answered.

Once she had cleared the drive of their estate, the crossing roads in all directions led to their land and the tenants who cared for it. Not knowing where he might be now, she had no choice but to start at the beginning of Mr. Easton's afternoon of chores.

She admitted she never thought him to be one for tenant chores. But then again, she would have never thought him to be one to turn his whole life upside down and marry a woman to rescue her from ruin. And yet here he was. She decided she might not ever be certain what to expect from the man and that might be a lovely positive to their marriage. The security of the word, marriage, was so much more the balm than she expected it to be.

The wind tickled her neck. The sun dappled everything around her, and she decided she much preferred the out of doors to any time inside. As she approached the Hendersons', voices made her smile. They obviously preferred the out of doors as well.

As soon as she came into sight around the bend, Mrs. Henderson waved her over. "Oh, it's her ladyship!" Her hand pumped the air in an excitement Dosie had never seen on the woman before. She slowed in front of their home. "And how are the Hendersons?"

"We are just excellent." A rosy faced Mrs. Henderson lined up her children just so and stood beside the mister.

"Pleased I am to hear it."

"And might we say, we are so happy to have our roof fixed."

"Oh, is it? Well and truly fixed?" She had doubted Mr. Easton's abilities. Of course she had. When does a gentleman learn how to mend roofs?

"Yes, your Mr. Easton." She fanned herself, much to the pretended annoyance of Mr. Henderson. Then she laughed. "He mended the roof good and tight and the door hinges besides." She smiled. "We sent him away with our best lard."

The pigs that roamed the place, inside and out, distracted her a moment. But they gifted her estate with the best hams so she would never complain. "I'm pleased to hear things are well here. And to see all your children. My they've grown."

"Yes they have. They're doing well in their studies."

"Excellent. Keep up the good work." She nudged her horse to keep walking. The next tenants were the Jolleys. Had Mr. Easton worked his magic there as well? The closer she came to their front door, the louder their family noises became, only these didn't sound as pleased as the last. She picked up her pace, hoping Mr. Easton hadn't gotten himself into a mess of a problem unawares. But as she moved closer, she saw that it was just Mr. Jolley, encouraging his son to chop the wood, but the boy was reluctant. She moved closer. "Oh. Mr. Jolley, Timothy. I love that work you are doing there. Is it possible young Timothy can cut through the wood?" She leaned forward. "It looks way too thick to me, is it possible that you can get that ax through a whole log?"

"Yes, ma'am. I can do it something with just one lowering of the ax."

"Really! Let's see now." She winked at his father.

The lad pulled up his sleeves, rubbed his hands together, swung the ax around behind him and let it fall on the wood. Split down the center.

"Why! You did it! I'm so amazed. Well done." Her smile grew as she looked at evidence of mending the porch.

"You see your good Mr. Easton has been here, helping us mend the porch. And he told Timothy here that the boy needed to split these logs before dark."

"Oh, you'll easily be able to accomplish that task. Judging from what I just saw." She dipped her head. "It is good to see you again. Give my regards to Mrs. Jolley."

"I will, my lady. She's resting after a long day."

"Did I hear her confinement would soon be over?"

"Yes, if we are so blessed, Timothy will have a little brother this time next month."

"Oh, that's excellent news indeed."

She moved on. And as she rode by tenant after tenant, mention of the glorious Mr. Easton came from every dwelling. Until she wondered if she'd miss him entirely. Right before the road she would take to turn back to the house, she could hear the pounding of a hammer. Perhaps she'd caught up to Mr. Easton at last.

Sure enough, as soon as the home came into view, Mr. Easton did as well, up in a tree. He had the footmen assisting and they were sitting on various branches in the tree with him. She laughed.

Mr. Easton whipped his head around and then smiled. His cravat was gone. His jacket off, the muscles on his arms visible through the thin fabric and his chest all but bare.

"Goodness, Mr. Easton." She felt her face go crimson.

"My apologies, my lady." His words were proper, but he didn't look apologetic at all. He looked so much like he'd never had as much enjoyment as he did climbing in a tree that she forgave him. "And what are you doing?"

"They're building me a tree fort." A small voice called up to her.

"Oh, well hello to you. Am I correct in guessing that you are one of the Williams' lads?"

"Yes, ma'am. I am Tony Williams. And I pulled up the biggest weed so I got to choose the next chore and this is it." He turned his grinning face back up to watch Mr. Easton.

"Ah, and are you an architect as well, Mr. Easton?"

"I am when I have such as this lad here to guide me." He dipped his head to Tony who stood taller. "They're almost done. Today we're just doing the first part which is the platform."

Mr. Easton tapped his feet on the wood beneath. "See this here? No one is falling out of this platform." He turned to the footman at his side. "Let's show her."

Her eyes widened as he and the footman, still dressed in his livery, jumped together on the platform. "See? Solid."

"I do see. Well done." She nodded in mock seriousness.

He turned. "We just have one more nail, right there." He tapped his hammer on a nail and then handed the tool to her footman. "That about does it." His hands left a trail of sawdust or dirt or something as he wiped them down his front. Then he climbed down, dropping the last five feet.

"What are you doing with your afternoon, Mr. Easton? You've left a train of happy tenants in your wake."

"Have I? For they've certainly given me much to be pleased over." He laid a hand on her horse and the gesture felt so intimate for a moment that she held her breath with wonder.

"You are quite flushed, Lady Theadosia. Are you well? Perhaps overheated?" He turned to reach for a bucket and ladle. "Would you care for a drink?"

She studied him and then shook her head. "I'm fine, thank you." What on earth had come over Mr. Easton? He seemed every bit as comfortable working with the tenants as he had in polite company. Perhaps her old friend was impressive as well as handsome? And to be her husband. Her heart trembled in happiness at the thought.

Chapter Fifteen

✾

osie found herself wanting to spend more time with
Mr. Easton. For a moment, she wished she had been
aiding the tenants at his side.

"We are about finished here for the day. Might I walk you
home?" He stepped up beside her horse.

"Certainly. I'll hop down and we can walk together."

"If you wish, or you may ride." He turned to the footmen.
"Thank you, Jacques and Henry. If you could, return the cart
and tools where they belong."

"Yes, Mr. Easton."

"You've turned our footmen into laborers."

"Are they not meant to labor?" His eyebrow wiggled, just
one, which made her laugh. "Besides, it was Mrs. Hamblin
that suggested them."

"Did she?" She shifted her body weight. "Perhaps you
could help me down?"

"Oh, of course. Please forgive my state of undress."

"Forgiven." Although certainly not forgotten. Her small
smile could not be concealed though she tried.

"What is this? Do you find me amusing, Lady Theadosia?"

At that, she could only laugh. "Not amusing, no."

He reached up and put his hands around her waist, lowering her slowly until she stood in front of him, the horse pressed up behind her. "Appealing."

"Hm?" His face was close. His words barely a murmur.

"Thank you."

"But before that, you said…appealing? You find me appealing?"

"Oh, if you must belabor the point." She could not hide the heat in her face.

"Not at all, but I do enjoy hearing it. So, should I dress this way around the house? Perhaps in the family wing?" He winked. "Parade about just for you?" His puffed out his chest.

And she could only laugh further. "Oh stop. If you like."

"I think I should like. Especially if you'll blush as you are now." He lifted her hand in his and brought the tips of her fingers to his lips. "So we're clear, I find you appealing too."

Her mouth dropped open. Then she closed it and forced a swallow. "Then we are in good stead."

He tucked her hand in his arm. "I quite agree with you there. Though I must make myself useful."

"Is this why you're out here helping the tenants?"

"Of course. And because it needed to be done. Mrs. Hamblin said they've been sending round petitions for assistance for a long time with no one to act." He shrugged. "I could only wander about the house alone for so many hours before I needed to make use of myself."

"Well, if this is the manner in which you entertain yourself, I'm certain all in the neighborhood will appreciate it." She walked in quiet for a moment. "Shall we attend the Hamilton house party?"

"Do you wish to?"

"Yes, most definitely. Lady Jane will be attending. And it is close enough we may sleep here or there. And they will have the fun of a decorated home and games and of course Twelfth Night."

"I love the sound of that." He rested a hand over her own. "And where would you like to marry?"

She sucked in her breath. He didn't know her well enough to guess if it was of surprise or disapproval or shock. But he waited for her response.

"I think we should marry wherever we like."

"Perhaps best to marry soon if I am to be living on your estate?"

"Perhaps you are correct. Though people are so senseless with this nonsense. You staying on the estate with people everywhere. What could be the harm in that?" She flipped her hands around when she talked. Especially when she was nervous, these habits came out.

"I can see a bit of sense in it."

"Can you?" She stopped. "And why is that? Is my reputation so terribly in danger with you here?"

He studied her beautiful face, her pert nose and the fit of her gown. His eyes travelled slowly over her face and along her neckline. Then he stepped closer. "I can see a good many reasons why a man could be a danger indeed."

"Oh." Her softly sighed response couldn't be helped. What indeed had come over her friend? The man with whom she'd only passed the time? Would he now engage in all manner of flirtations with her? She wouldn't complain if he did.

She cleared her throat. "We have a chapel in the house. Many of my ancestors have been married there. I would be pleased to do the same."

"That sounds wonderful. I have acquired the special license. Edward had it sent on ahead of us by express rider. We can do so any day."

"Perhaps we invite the vicar."

"Yes, I think he is a necessary piece."

She laughed. "And Mother."

"Yes, another necessary member."

"I'm uncertain when my father shall join us."

He nodded. "When does Lady Jane arrive?"

"Oh, how good of you to think of her. Yes, I would most like her to attend. I expect directly. She has an estate nearby. Perhaps I shall send a note round to her mother."

"Excellent." He hummed along beside her.

"I'm wondering, if you would like to meet me in the library for breakfast tomorrow?"

"Oh, that sounds lovely!" She tipped her head back to look up into his face. "Are you…courting me, Mr. Easton?"

"I am, my lady." He mock bowed. "Don't you think that if a man wants to marry a woman, he should court her first?"

"That usually comes first, yes." She stepped lightly, a great pleasure at the thought rising up inside. "But I will be grateful for what you did, always, proper courtship or not."

"Someday, perhaps, I will resent that gratitude and wish for something more." He stared straight ahead but his words went to her heart. Then he looked down into her face. "But for now, I will take it, for I know I am undeserving, unworthy in every way of you."

She was shaken. How could that be? "I…"

"Say no more. We don't need to think more on it. But know this. The gratitude is mine."

"Then we are both to be forever grateful?" She laughed.

"Not a bad place to be, but perhaps, my beautiful almost wife…"

She sucked in a breath.

"Perhaps. We can be something more." His eyes held promises. His mouth quirked up just enough and a hint of fire in his face excited her to the tips of her toes.

They walked along in quiet for many steps until she said simply, "Perhaps." She began to think it the greatest desire of her heart.

That evening, after a lengthy and comfortable conversation in the library, he asked to walk her to her room.

She stood and rested a hand on his arm. The air between them felt charged with anticipation. What on earth for, she couldn't know. Perhaps knowing they would be married increased anticipation. Perhaps her knowing he slept next door, with a bit of wood between their two living spaces was doing things to her already enamored heart. Tingles rushed through her. She stood closer, her arm at his side.

They walked through the halls, the rooms, and then up the stairs saying very little. Did he feel all that she did? She pursed her lips.

His gaze moved there. And then she smiled. "My room is here." She stopped in front of her door.

"Next to mine." He stared into her face. "With a door inside?"

She nodded, slowly. "These are another set of master bedchambers. We thought it helpful to get us situated where we would be. Are your rooms to your liking?"

"Yes, certainly. I'm quite comfortable. And I noticed the door." He smiled, suddenly roguish. "I tried the handle."

She laughed, grateful for a respite from the intensity. But she stepped closer. "And what if it had not been locked?"

He ran a finger from her shoulder to the top of her palm, sending a shower of needy expectation. "Then I would have seen your bedchamber. Sadly, I don't think you were in it at the time."

"Hm. One day I will be."

"I've thought of that."

"Have you?"

He raised her hand to his lips, but then shook his head when they found the soft material of her glove, covering the skin on the back of her hand. "This won't do." He tugged at each finger until the whole of it slid from her hand and dropped on the floor. The lips he placed on her soft and sensitive fingers were playful, nibbling, and fun. He turned her hand over, running a line of kisses into her palm. "I should say goodnight."

"No." She laughed at her response, sudden as it was.

"No?" His gaze caressed her face. "So you like this?"

She nodded.

He pressed his lips to the inside of her wrist. "And this?"

Her hand reached forward, resting on the front of his jacket. "Very much."

Before she knew what was happening, she was in his arms, his strength holding her gently. He kissed the top of her head and then stepped back. "I think you and I shall have a fine time of things, don't you?"

"I think we shall. Thank you again, Mr. Easton, for rescuing me."

"More gratitude?"

She shook her head. "Well, yes, but I think of you more as those knights in my books, as those lovers in my stories who see a maiden in distress and rescue her from harm. Not gratitude as much as some sort of starry eyed...something." Had she just spoken all of that out loud? To Mr. Easton? She dipped her head. "You must think me addled. I'm sorry."

"No, your words are magic to my ears. And I will attempt to earn not your gratitude, starry eyed though it is, and more your love."

She sucked in a breath. He'd said the word, love. But she could only hope the same. "Good night, Mr. Easton."

"Call me Julian."

"And me, Dosie."

A new intimacy settled between them, one that she hoped might linger.

Chapter Sixteen

✿❀✿

J ulian continued his work for the tenants the next day
with thoughts full of Dosie. He'd wanted to kiss her full
and delicious looking mouth more than he should
have. But he couldn't be more pleased that they
seemed suited. That a flirtation with her had been easy and
natural, that he indeed found himself more and more
wishing to be at her side. They each attended to what
amounted to chores. Dosie sat with the housekeeper and
then with her mother most of the afternoon. He felt something couples must feel when both are working for their
home.

But as he pulled in at the main house, his chin opened, his
body dirty and tired, a carriage arrived at the front door.
Knowing he looked like a servant, he turned to the side in the
direction to make his way around back toward the stables but
paused at the corner of the house, curious.

When Standish stepped out of the equipage impatiently
waving aside his servants, Julian leaped from the cart. "Take
care of this, Jacques."

He rushed in through the front door as Lord Standish was
being shown into the front room.

"What's this?" Julian burst in behind him, ignoring all semblance of ceremony or manners.

"Mr. Easton." Hansen looked as though he would say something but then closed his mouth.

"Please stay in the room with Lord Standish until he leaves us."

The man stiffened. "Am I not to be trusted in the front parlor?"

"Forgive me, but no." He turned to Hansen. "This man forced himself upon Lady Theadosia. I'm certain she would find his presence unwelcome. I am only humoring him as I would like to hear him state his case." Mr. Easton approached, standing in front of the interloper.

"I'm merely here to make my apologies, if you must know." Something about the man seemed weasley still, but such a request would be granted. He nodded to Hansen, and the obviously perplexed servant turned to leave.

"She will be down in a moment if she deems your request worth her time."

As soon as they were mostly alone, Standish sneered. "I don't know what you are still so unhappy about. You've benefitted quite nicely from my error."

"We will not be discussing my situation in this manner."

"And why not? Edward forcing you to marry, you coming upon the lovely Lady Theadosia at just the right time to cover all your gambling debts. Does she know her dowry will be used to pay off half the ton? Does she know that Edward gave you such an ultimatum?"

"What?" Dosie stood in the doorway.

Julian was too unsettled at first to respond appropriately, and he could do nothing about the unworthiness he felt that was surely visible across his face. He shook his head. "Dosie, no."

"Edward made you marry me?"

Lord Standish snorted. "Does she think this is a love

match?" He tipped his head back. "Oh, my dear. The only difference between him and me is that he's easier to look at."

"No." She stepped further into the room. "He never forced himself upon me."

Lord Standish lifted a shoulder. "I have come to apologize. I quite forgot myself in an emotional grab for your hand. I blame my enamored heart and nothing more." His dead-panned face, his emotionless response was confusing at best. But Dosie reached out her hand.

Julian stepped forward with a jerk, but realized he couldn't prevent the man from touching her hand.

"We shall forget it ever happened. Especially now as I will be married and hopefully you as well, in the not distant future."

He nodded, then straightened his jacket. "Thank you for your time. I leave much lighter in my concern about my behavior. May I wish you every happiness?"

"Yes, thank you."

Julian stepped to her side, in all his disarray.

They stood together until Lord Standish had left the house. Then Dosie waved to the servants. "Please leave us for a moment and shut the door."

As soon as they were alone, her eyes blazed. "You lied to me?"

"What? I never did."

"Edward forced this marriage?"

"No. He most certainly did not. He was of course happy about it. But now…" He shook his head for so long even he didn't believe what came out of his mouth, though it was true. "I stepped in to marry you because you needed help. Plain and simple. I came the next morning because I wanted to do my duty by you even though I felt unworthy. Edward convinced me that you would think highly of me because I was rescuing you. So I carried forward our plan of ensuring your father saw reason, by law and by your own request."

She lifted her chin. "But you didn't wish to marry."

"Of course not. Not right away." He stared her down. "Did you?"

When she looked away, he knew he could continue. Her indecisive expressions were her most obvious.

"You knew as well as I that the whole situation was not perhaps the hoped-for result of a ball."

"And now you're stuck with me, forced by your brother."

He shook his head. "I would never step away. I'm honor and duty bound, but it's not just that."

Her lip trembled.

"What? No, Dosie. Please, come here." He tried to embrace her, but she stepped away. "I see what you mean about gratitude being a loathsome word. I feel the same about duty and honor."

He raised a hand to reach for her again but then dropped it. "Would you have me be dishonorable?"

The expression she turned to him was pained and full of passion. "For love? Yes. I'd have you lose duty for love, not be the recipient of your duty-bound obligations."

"Just as I wish to lose your gratitude for love."

They took each other's measure. Julian could see her shoulders set and the yearning in her eyes turn to the practicality he usually saw there. "Then we will move forward best we can."

"Yes, and I hope our feelings will grow…"

"Of course." She waved him off and left the room in a hurry. So quickly, he was left with only her lingering scent of lilacs to tease his senses.

***

Later that night, his mind still on Standish, a noise outside his window brought him standing in the moonlight on his balcony. He couldn't get rid of the ominous concern that Standish was not giving up, that he would try something more. He saw intruders in every tree, every shadow out on the grounds. The form moved in the darkness near him on the balcony.

"Who's there?"

Dosie stepped out of the shadows.

A long breath of relief escaped. "Do we share a balcony?" He stepped closer. "I haven't been out here enough to notice."

"Yes." She wrapped her arms around herself as her night-shift swayed in the breeze.

"Dosie, I…"

"No, don't say more. Of course, our marriage will not be the ideal. I should not expect otherwise."

"But it can be. The beginning is quite the fairytale adventure story, and the middle quite nice, I will admit, but the ending, the ending can be the most powerful of all." He stepped as near as he dared.

She stood as still as he'd ever seen her, her face still in the shadows. He had no guesses as to her thoughts, but he hoped she would take comfort.

"I've been a cad in my life. I've been a financial mess. You saw me at the ball. I've tried desperately to erase that memory from your mind. I had come from a night of waste and drunken idiocy." He shook his head. "But I did one right thing."

She lifted her chin.

"I offered to marry you." He turned to look out over the expanse of the estate. "And it has nothing to do with my money or this beautiful estate or your father's influence…it's you."

"What?" She stepped nearer.

"Yes, you. You are the reason for me now. And marriage or not. I'd like the opportunity to court you properly." The words came out unplanned, but he meant every one of them. He turned back to see her reaction. "Might we try again? Would you allow me to earn even your love?"

She stepped into the light, her eyes welling with tears. "I'd like that."

He nodded. "Your heart is yours to give. And I'd consider myself unworthily blessed if you were to ever share it with me."

She reached a hand out.

He took her chilled fingers in his hand and kissed them once. Then bowed to her and shut the door to his room before he thought too much longer on her only partially dressed form.

Sleep came slowly but pleasantly as he began plans to woo his intended.

But the next morning he was awoken by screams. "It's her ladyship! He's taken her ladyship!"

He shot out of bed, meeting her mother in the hall. Her face was drawn, stricken with worry. "She's gone." Her hand clenched at her nightdress.

"I will find her." He shouted over his shoulder and he shoved his feet into boots while running.

As soon as he saw a servant, he shouted, "What has happened?"

"Her ladyship has gone missing from the stables. Lord Standish's carriage was seen riding north at fast speeds."

He tore out the door. "I need a team of footmen. Also, call the magistrate."

"His lordship is the magistrate." Her mother clutched the railing above them with white knuckled hands.

He stopped. "Lord Hunting?"

"Yes. You now. You be the magistrate in his place."

JULIAN DIDN'T KNOW IF HE COULD DO THAT, BUT IF IT MEANT reaping justice all over Lord Standish, then so be it. "I will do whatever it takes. You have my word."

She nodded. And the trust in her eyes further strengthened him.

He raced for the stables, swing up onto his already saddled horse, shouted thank you, and took off on the road to Scotland.

She would not marry that criminal creep. She would not be forced by his hand. She would not… All manner of other atrocities crowded into his brain of all the things she would not. His horse ran faster, as if spurred by Julian's own panic.

They raced up the road, dodging carriages and carts and other forms of conveyance. He must find her, must stop their race before any of the unthinkables happened.

Chapter Seventeen

✦❧✦

Dosie fought against the rope at her wrists, but it only
served to rub at her raw skin. "You will certainly
pay for this." Her arms were pulled behind her, tied
tight. Her feet were free and her mouth was free, but her
shoulders had begun to ache and the skin at her wrists stung
from her constant movement in the carriage, bracing herself
against falling. The carriage rocked and bounced from the
precarious speed over uneven roads. She knew they were
headed north. She knew he hoped for the anvil in Scotland to
force her hand. But that was utterly ridiculous as her father
would denounce it all. But she would be well and truly ruined,
taken. Would Julian want her still? She swallowed her fright.
Of course he would. If he knew soon enough, he might be on
his way in pursuit, but how could he even discover her
absence?

Lord Standish sat across from her on the other side of the
carriage. "Oh, I think I'll be the one to be paid." He'd asked
his thugs to ride outside with the coachman, thankfully or
she'd have been bouncing around against all manner of men.
As it was, riding in the small space alone with Lord Standish
was, of course, particularly loathsome.

"What do you mean you'll be paid? Certainly not by me."

"I mean, someone will pay me for your hand, someone will pay me if we marry. Someone will pay me simply because you are in my possession. You are a valuable asset no matter how this turns out."

"I can't believe my father was originally inclined to give you my hand. He certainly won't be in support now." She gritted her teeth in her extreme frustration.

"Oh, he would have done nearly anything for the chance at another vote in the houses of Parliament. Spread a rumor about my father and suddenly, the word is open for a profitable marriage."

"Is your father not even going to become a duke?" She gasped.

"He might. He is talking with the prince." He flicked something off his knee. "The opportunity is perhaps not as certain as people were led to believe."

"And you won't be able to show your face in the ton ever again!"

"Why not? Who would you want to tell about this shame and ruin?"

She opened her mouth and then closed it. What an evil and well-designed plan. She wanted nothing more than to wipe the self-satisfied sneer off his face. But she had no recourse, no strength left and no one near who could help.

***

Julian rode his horse until the animal was frothing at the mouth and still Julian had not caught sight of Lord Standish's carriage. "Come on. Come on!" He kept calling to his horse. The good animal kept pushing until at last, something up ahead caught his eye. The black of a carriage as it made a turn, a bit of dust on the road, way ahead at the top of the incline.

He leaned forward and they pushed farther. When at last they were in sight and hearing, he saw why he had trouble keeping up. The coach flew at dangerous speeds over these roads. Their coachman whipped the horses while the animals raced on ever narrower roads. They were all at risk. As he moved closer, they hadn't yet noticed him. Likely each man clung for his very life. Turning corners, taking up the whole of the road when someone else could be coming the opposite direction. Racing up upon another carriage that might move slower to their front. Many things could go amiss at those speeds and his heart pounded harder with every sway and dip and turn up ahead. He must get to Dosie before she was put at further risk.

Standish had men holding onto the outside of the carriage, large, armed men.

And Julian realized the foolishness of his plan to ride on ahead alone before anyone else on the estate. He had no choice at this point but to follow behind and wait for an opportunity. The carriage dipped in ruts, the wheels taking it, the spring holding, but Julian didn't know for how long. He hoped and he watched, ready.

His horse was starting to slow. Keeping up at this speed, finding sure footing was getting harder in the growing darkness. Julian didn't know how long he could keep this up. And he knew no one would be catching up to them, not until they stopped.

As his horse stumbled for the second time, Julian knew he had to make his move. He approached closer in behind the carriage, considering his options. Just as he was about to shout, "Stand and deliver," the carriage hit a rather deep rut, upsizing one end while the other went low, but the wheel never recovered. The carriage pushed forward into the rut and upended on itself. Before Julian could think another thing, the whole equipage was rolling end over end, his chest seizing in panic.

He raced toward the overturned carriage, wrenched open the door, and breathed out in relief that the only opened eyes staring back at him were hers. He reached in and pulled her to him in the most desperately hopeful embrace he'd ever experienced. He lifted her from her feet and carried her from the carriage. "Are you well? Are you really well?"

She nodded but said nothing. Her body trembled in his arms.

"Hold it right there." The click of a pistol sounded behind him and a voice he didn't recognize.

He turned slowly.

"I think you're taking something that belongs to Standish."

"What? His boots?" Julian pretended to study his boots while holding Dosie. "Nope. I have none of his possessions."

"Put her down and walk away slowly."

Julian shook his head. "I just don't think I can do that."

The man raised the pistol to eye level, pointing it straight at him.

But Julian frowned. "You gonna shoot the woman? She's worth nothing to you dead."

He raised his pistol still further until it was likely pointed at Julian's head. "Do it now."

"It's fine. Put me down." She wiggled.

But he adjusted his hold on her and murmured. "No."

Servants who had been flung from the carriage were starting to move. Some were caught underneath. Some had been thrown over the top and were in the road up ahead. He didn't want to know what had happened to their magnificent and abused horses.

Someone crawled out of the carriage door.

Julian put her down, but kept her directly in front of him. "I'm going to untie your ropes."

She stiffened when he touched her raw wrists but nodded. He gritted his teeth at the evidence of mistreatment he saw near her hands.

Standish made his way toward them, stumbling, clutching

at his own arm which hung at an unnatural angle from his body.

Julian at last freed her from the ropes. "You need to run."

"No. They'll shoot you."

"Just do it."

"I won't leave you."

Julian's sigh was loud. "That's it, Standish. She says she doesn't want to marry you."

Standish sneered. "I don't remember caring too much about what she wants."

Movement behind him caught Julian's eye.

"But we do care about that sort of thing." A voice atop a horse came closer. Jacques, Julian's now favorite footman. And a group of other servants and men he didn't know.

"From the village." Dosie's whisper sounded stronger.

Standish whirled around, facing them. "This is nothing for you to concern yourself over."

More men arrived, a whole group of them, carrying guns. "We're concerned whenever anyone treats horses the way you have." He waved a hand and two of his men approached the horses. They were hidden from Julian's sight behind the carriage, and must be laying prone. He hoped some of them could be saved.

"And we concern ourselves with the apparent abduction of women." He rode closer. "You being abducted, ma'am?"

She nodded. "Yes, by that man and all his men. I was trapped in that carriage."

"You Easton?" He nodded at Julian.

"I am, sir, thank you."

"I hear you're the acting Magistrate in place of Lord Hunting."

"I am, yes."

"We received an express rider not long ago, warning us of their arrival, stating that you might need some support."

Julian breathed out in relief. "Yes, thank you." He nodded

to the men, standing taller. To Dosie he murmured, "Praise your mother."

Dosie reached a hand to lean on him and he realized her weakened state. He swiftly lifted her up into his arms.

"We have rooms for you at the inn and for all the others. They'll go before my court in the morning."

"Thank you," Dosie called out.

"You're very welcome."

His men made quick work of freeing those trapped by the carriage, of assisting men to their feet and tying men with ropes. Standish lashed out when they approached him. "My father is the duke of Albany."

"Not yet, he's not."

Standish was tied up and fabric shoved into his mouth. "I figure you've heard enough words from this man." The man looked to Dosie.

"Yes, sir." Her voice was shaky, but her smile was large and sincere.

She rode in front of him on his horse. They took the pace slow, to save the horse and to allow their hearts to slow and the confidence of their safety to settle around them.

His arms circled her, as if to shield her from any other harmful thing.

"If I say thank you, will you be displeased?"

He laughed. "No. My dear, dear Dosie, no. You will never displease me again. I shall look at you every day happy you are indeed well and mine. Shall we marry tomorrow?" He was kidding, but only just.

She laughed in response but leaned back into him as though to stay permanently, which he was perfectly happy about.

In short order, Julian was standing outside her room at the inn and they were preparing for sleep.

"Julian."

He loved the sound of his name on her lips.

"Please, sleep in my room."

He couldn't stop the quick grin that filled his face.

"Oh stop, come in. I'm petrified Standish or his men will try again. They're here somewhere in the same inn."

He adjusted his smile. "I'm just enjoying a bit of a tease. Certainly, I will sleep in the chair by the window." He stepped closer, looking into her eyes hoping his sincerity would show. "No one will be able to harm you again." He meant his words. He'd never felt so urgent about any task. If they had hurt her, he would have been destroyed.

"Thank you." Her great relief at the thought that he would be near filled him with such a sense of purpose, with pride, with love even, that he at last felt truly useful to the woman.

When he closed the door, he led her to her bed. She climbed in and he pulled the covers up to her chin. "Goodnight, almost wife." He kissed her forehead.

"Goodnight, almost husband."

She looked so young, so innocent in that bed, that Julian vowed to be even better than he had been to deserve her. For the first time in a long time, he felt a sense of wholeness. He brought something to their union just as she did and together they would be one. He pulled his chair closer to the bed but still between her and the window, leaned back and closed his eyes. He might not sleep much, but he would enjoy every moment of his vigil, knowing that because she had him, she could sleep well that night.

He did sleep remarkably well and when the roosters started crowing, he felt somewhat rested. He awoke to her large eyes staring at him from under her bedcovers.

"Well, look who's awake." He smiled, his feelings tender.

"You're handsome when you sleep."

"You're beautiful all the time, but most especially right now." He was filled with a sudden desire to scoop her up and kiss her senseless. Soon enough he could kiss those heavy eyelids and leave a trail along her neck. He stopped his thoughts, knowing that direction would serve no purpose.

"What are you thinking?"

He coughed, then paused, caught in his thoughts. But searching her face and seeing the flash of wicked enjoyment in her eyes, he chose boldness. "I was thinking about how desperately I want to place my lips on your eyes, your mouth, your neck, you..."

"Stop." Her face flamed red. "Thank you. I understand." She sat up, holding covers to her chest. "How will we travel home?"

"We can rent horses, or a carriage, or..." He'd been giving this whole scenario some thought while he dozed in the chair.

"Or?"

"Once that cretin took off with you in his clutches, I immediately regretted not marrying you straight away. Once we're married, you hold no more temptation for him or others."

"And we're this close to Scotland?"

"Precisely. We're this close to Scotland." He cleared his throat. "It's not the wedding you hoped for in the chapel at your estate."

"No, it's not, but could we not repeat something there? After the fact?"

"We could absolutely repeat something even more special there." She was much more amenable to this suggestion than he thought she'd be.

Chapter Eighteen

Dosie knew the reason she was supportive of the Scotland idea had nothing to do with her own concerns for safety. Once Standish was locked away, no one else posed a threat to her. But watching Julian sleep, having him in her room all night and awaking to his handsome face awoke her to another of the joys of marriage. And she was suddenly impatient to begin. But marry across the anvil? She laughed at her own thoughts. Was there really a need to rush off to Scotland?

Then her door burst open. "She's my daughter and I'll enter when I want!" Her father stood in the doorway, his face ashen, his hair disheveled. "My Theodosia." He ran to her and scooped her in his arms.

She couldn't remember the last time, or any time, he'd hugged her. He just didn't do things like that. But now, he clutched her to him as though she were something precious and the realization brought immediate tears to her eyes. "Father?"

"Oh, Dosie. I almost lost you. This is all my fault. I should have never alerted that awful man as to your dowry." He shook his head. "Forgive me?"

She nodded. "Of course. Julian saved me. Twice now. I am well. Mama is well. Perhaps we could spend Christmas on our estate?"

"Of course, anything. We'll even visit that Hamilton house party if you like."

"Perhaps we shall. Julian's brothers will be there."

"And Tabitha and Henry too." Julian called over to them.

"Mr. Easton." Her father reached a hand to him, indicating he should approach. "I owe you a huge debt of gratitude. If not for you..." He wiped at his face. "I would have lost a daughter. For who knows what that man would have done once they were married." He pulled Julian closer and suddenly Dosie was wrapped in the arms of her father and her almost husband and she didn't think life could be any sweeter.

"I think we should marry in your chapel." Julian didn't know where the words had come from or why this particular timing, but Dosie nodded, her eyes misty from tears. "Yes, tomorrow."

They all laughed but father and groom both answered at the same time. "Yes."

***

Dosie walked down the aisle of their ancient chapel on the arm of her father.

He whispered, "I'm so proud of you, Dosie."

"Even with things as they are? Forced into marriage?"

"He is a good man we would have chosen ourselves, is he not?"

She looked ahead to his joyful face. "He is, the best of men."

"You kept things going right even when I was losing sight of all that's really important."

"You were doing important things too, Father."

"Nothing as important as you." He wiped at his eyes.

Her heart felt full to bursting. The chapel was full of friends and neighbors. Lady Jane was there. All the Eastons and their sister and husband were there. Lord Hamilton was there, demanding they attend his house party as a newly married couple. Dosie had readily agreed and Julian's response? "My, you really love house parties."

The chapel was filled with greenery. Holly, boughs, berries everywhere you looked, and of course, mistletoe. And on the ground, for as far as the eye could see? Snow.

As requested, their vicar read from the Christmas story in Luke chapter two as a part of their ceremony. Perhaps it was because of the smallness of the room or perhaps the intimate feeling of the group of loved ones, or her growing love for Julian, but Dosie had never experienced such a thick and encompassing feeling of peace and warmth as was in the chapel with them. It was almost as if the angels from the birth of Jesus had come to join them and sing their carols from on high. When it at last came time for her to take him as her husband, her yes rang out across the chapel in a strong, clear tone. His resounded with a beautiful reverence. And then in an uncharacteristic moment of boldness, the vicar said, "You may kiss your bride."

Mr. Easton's eyes lit and Dosie could only laugh. But he pulled her close immediately and stared down into her face. The tenderness there, the love, filled her soul to almost bursting. "I love you." His breath tickled her lips as the words filled her soul.

"I love you too." His lips covered hers in a moment of unity like none she'd ever known and then they parted. Breathless, she turned to wave at the cheering room full of people. They hurried by in the midst of them all, waving and laughing. When the doors opened, the entire courtyard was filled with all the people from the nearby village. "The tenants!" Julian shouted. "Oh, it's good to see you!"

He dug in his purse for the money bag and threw coins into the air.

Dosie waved and called to them all, catching rice in her hair and all around them. They climbed aboard an open phaeton and rode through their cheering happy faces and down the drive.

"Whew!" She laughed. "That was amazing! Such dear friends. Can you believe all the tenants came?"

"Of course they came!" He smiled, holding the reins. "And now, off to the hunter's cabin?"

"Yes." Her gaze slid to his. "They set it up for us." Suddenly shy, she had nothing more to say about their upcoming evening. In truth, she wasn't certain what to expect.

"Shall I take this road then, and follow it around and through the woods?"

"Yes, we used to play there as children."

"Excellent. You'll have to show me all the spots to hide."

She laughed.

"Are you expecting to need to hide?"

"You never know with you."

"Very funny."

His gentle teasing put her at ease so much that by the time they arrived in front of the hunter's cabin she was excited for their meal.

"Would you look at that." He pointed upward.

Someone had built a tree fort in the tree out front. And in it, was a package.

"How ingenious! Do you think it was the tenants?"

"Certainly. I'd recognize that handiwork anywhere."

"Let us take a look, shall we?" She turned to get a closer look.

"Excellent."

He leapt off and hurried around to her then lifted his hands. "May I assist you?"

"Yes." She put her hands on his shoulders and he lowered

her to stand in front of him. Her body filled with a new sense of wild expectation. "Come on, then." She tugged his hand. They climbed up into the tree fort. She managed with his help, even as she bunched her skirts in one hand and held them close. They sat together, the package in between them.

"Open it then." He pushed it toward her.

She tugged at the strings and the brown wrapping fell open. Inside was a music box, with beautiful inlaid wood and a lovely carving of a pair of birds. "It's lovely!"

She lifted the lid. Inside was a note. "What's this, do you suppose?"

The paper unfolded to Julian's handwriting. "From you?"

"Yes, the box was my mother's. It's one of the few things of hers that I was able to keep."

"Oh, it's even more lovely. Thank you." She read the letter.

My dearest Dosie,

We entered into this marriage in an unconventional manner certainly, but I am falling in love with you the way our parents fell in love with each other and I wish to keep my promise to court you, even in marriage. I wish to earn your heart and your trust. Consider this the beginning of a lifetime of courtship.

My love always,

Julian

"I didn't know anyone could be so happy." She laughed. "Thank you."

"Now." He twisted around on their platform. "How to get you down from here."

"And why should we climb down?"

"Wish to sleep up here, do you?"

"Well, no."

"And the food smells divine."

They eased their way to the ladder on the tree and she lifted her skirts to climb down. There was a moment of unease when she couldn't see the first rung on the ladder, but once her foot felt around a bit near the trunk, she was able to navigate the rest of the way down.

He followed shortly after with the box and letter under one arm.

They made their way to the front door and he scooped her up and held her close. "Our evening awaits, Mrs. Easton."

"Oh, I love the sound of that."

"More than my lady?"

"Most certainly. Mrs. Easton means always that I am with you."

He carried her up and into the cabin.

Everything looked so cozy. A fire was lit, dinner was set out, and a delicious smell filled the room.

"This is wonderful." She made her way to the table. "Shall we eat?"

"I was hoping you'd be hungry."

"Of course." She indicated he should sit next to her.

On his plate was a wrapped package.

"What is this?"

"Open it. Let's see."

He tugged at the string and it fell open on his plate.

A watch with a chain. He lifted it.

"Open it."

He did and inside was a tiny miniature of Dosie. She held her breath. Would he like it?

The gaze he lifted to her face shone with appreciation. "You got me a gift?"

"Of course I did. And now, no matter the time, you can know I'll be thinking of you."

He leaned across the table and kissed her.

She knew it was a spontaneous reaction and she loved it all the more because of it. But the moment his lips touched hers, she felt a fire rage inside, a sudden desire and need she'd never felt before. She leaned closer, unsure how to respond. Her lips sought his more and closer. She reached her hand to the back of his neck, holding him close.

He responded gently to her urgency, softly to her insistence, until he paused. And looked deeply into her eyes. "I love you."

"I love you too." Her breath came out in uneven spurts, her body trembled. But she swallowed and turned to their food. She cleared her throat. "This is my favorite meal."

"Oh? Let's see what Dosie loves to eat, shall we?"

While he lifted lids to pots and began serving for both of them, she downed her entire cup of wine and poured another.

They ate until neither could swallow another bite and then he led her over to the fire. "Let's read."

Ordinarily, she would have thought reading a most providential suggestion, but this evening, she thought more on those kisses.

Nevertheless, he opened up a book of Shakespeare's sonnets. And soon she was lost to the beautiful language and rhythm of his poetry.

Her gaze wandered. They had decorated the cottage with all manner of festive Christmas additions. And in the corner stood a tree, a full tree. She put her hand on Julian's arm. "Shall we decorate our Christmas tree?"

He followed her gaze. "Certainly." A box of items to place on the tree rested underneath its green boughs. "But let's make a game of it. Every ornament placed earns a kiss." His grin melted her insides. How could she have known Mr. Easton would be all she'd ever wanted in a husband?

"I'll go first." She eagerly reached for a toy horse and hung it on a high branch then turned to Julian.

He tucked a hair behind her ear. "You are a wonder to me, Dosie." His thumb ran along her lower lip, teasing, until she was almost overcome with desire for more of his lips on hers. He moved closer, his mouth hovering above her own, and then he covered her mouth. His lips were soft but this time more insistent, and she responded the best she knew how, loving him, enjoying him. He paused. His smile growing. "We'll never get this tree decorated."

"Those are lots of kisses." She grinned.

"Hm. And do you like kisses?"

Her nod was immediate.

One by one, they placed the ornaments until the whole of the green was embellished by the festive homespun creations and Dosie's lips were swollen and well kissed, her hair slightly mussed and her body humming.

"Let's do this every year."

"The first of our Julian and Dosie Easton family traditions."

They made their way to the upstairs bedrooms. He walked her to the door of one bedchamber. "This is where I say goodnight."

She stepped closer. "What are you doing?"

"I'm saying goodnight."

"Oh?" She studied his face. Did he not wish to do what married couples did? Perhaps he wasn't wanting that from her? Confusion muddled her hopeful expectation.

"I promised to court you and that includes waiting until we're ready for things to move along in this part of our relationship."

She thought his attempt at nobility was gentlemanly. She nodded. "I'll see you in the morning then?"

He nodded. Kissed her forehead and then turned to enter his own room.

But the rooms inside were connected by a door.

Dosie's maid stepped out of their closet.

"Oh good, Lucy, you're here. Now we must hurry and get me ready for Mr. Easton before he falls asleep."

She giggled. "I'm guessing there's not much sleeping happening over there."

"What? Lucy, really."

"Beggin' your pardon, ma'am."

"Oh, you're forgiven, let's hurry now!"

Lucy dressed Dosie in her loveliest night shift and brushed out her hair, plaiting it in an appealing side braid. Then she added some of her favorite waters to refresh her smell and sent her barefoot to the door that separated their rooms.

Epilogue

❧❧❧

A few days after their return from the hunting cottage, Julian and Dosie arrived in front of Lord Hamilton's home, full of excitement. Dosie looked as though she could hardly contain herself.

Julian shook his head. "You love a good house party."

"I certainly do. I'm so happy we could come." Her feet danced in place where she stood.

"Yes, I see that." He laughed.

Dosie was a light to his every day. She brought an energy and a love to everything they did, something that had brought him every happiness. He lifted her hand in his, pressing his lips against her glove. "As soon as we can, we are losing these gloves."

Her grin widened. And they stepped inside.

Their guests were gathering for the yearly tradition to play charades. "Oh, Julian. We have to win."

"Is Oscar here yet?"

"Your brother?"

"Yes, as long as he isn't here, we will win. I'm an expert when it comes to this game."

"But Oscar beats you?"

"Every time."

A man who looked like Julian, and she knew from her wedding to be Oscar, but had grown considerably since seeing him as a child, reached for her hand. "I'm going to need that in writing. He may never admit to such a thing again."

She offered it and he bowed. "Good to see you again, sister." He turned to the side. "You remember Tauney and Edward."

"Yes, thank you, Mr. Easton for stepping in to save my every happiness."

"It was my pleasure, believe me. And call me Edward. We are siblings now." He kissed her cheek, a move that shocked Julian but he took in stride.

"Thank you, Edward. I will." Her smile and ease with his brothers was another source of marital happiness to Julian. Who knew when he'd met Dosie that he was marrying another Easton. It was as if she'd been raised with them all.

Dosie smiled at all the guests who were gathering in the Hamilton great hall. A lovely blonde woman who seemed to exude light joined them. "Are we doing re-introductions? I'm Tabitha. Perhaps you will remember me as the one who looked somewhat like a young girl but acted so very much like my brothers." She grimaced. "I'm so pleased to at last have another woman in the family."

"What's wrong with all brothers, Tabby cat?" Tauney stepped up beside her.

She grinned. "I'm still called by my childhood nickname for one." She embraced Dosie. "Welcome to the family."

"Thank you." Dosie decided she loved her new sister completely.

They made their way into the drawing room where charades was just getting organized. "Prepare to lose." Oscar rolled his neck around and adjusted his sleeves.

"One of these days Oscar, you will lose at something." Tabitha shook her head.

They played long into the night. Lord Hamilton surprised them all with a pointed excellence at the game. Toward the end, Dosie and Oscar both had furrowed brows and barely spoke except to strategize. They'd created some sort of understood team, determined to beat Lord Hamilton.

Oscar stood at the front next. He walked with arms flapping at his side.

"Chicken!" Dosie shouted.

He pointed at her. Then he held something above his head and mimed kissing a woman.

"Mistletoe."

The others couldn't keep up. Dosie and Oscar were a two-person game.

Oscar then pretended to play cards and lose. Dosie guessed over and over but he ignored her. He moved on to being chastised by someone.

"Fight, argue, disagree."

Oscar waved her off. He then stood tall, approached Dosie and went down on one knee, his pleading face comical.

"Proposal. Marriage."

Oscar pointed and then spread his arms out and repeated each scene. Dosie was flummoxed. What was the man getting at?

Then Julian joined him, adding more. He pretended to build something.

"Hammer, build."

He climbed a ladder. "Tree. Tree fort!"

He pointed at her and nodded.

His next move, he sat as though on a horse. Then he pretended to fight someone. His arms were swinging. He ducked then scooped someone up in his arms.

"Aha!" She laughed. She ran up to the front and joined the other two. She placed arms as though tied behind her back and acted as though she were in great distress. Then free, pantomimed great gratitude, then a kiss, then marriage, walking down the aisle, then, with hands at her belly, cradling something precious, she stood in front of Julian.

"Stomachache? Illness? Your mother!"

She shook her head, and Oscar groaned.

Then Dosie cradled something in her arms, rocking and cooing.

Julian swept her in his arms, everyone else in the room forgotten. "Baby," he whispered.

She nodded.

Their kiss was received by much cheering and laughter and someone calling out, "Kiss."

**Read on for the first chapters of another book featuring the entire Easton family.

In the Quiet Before Delicious Mayhem Begins

Damen, most valued footman of the Countess du Breven, walked precisely three steps behind his employer, cradling her dog in his arms.

She waved impatiently but kept at her slow pace. "Come Damen, I insist upon personally inspecting each of the rooms before our guests arrive."

Of all the ridiculous notions. "Shall we visit all 365 rooms before tea?"

She lifted her chin. "I hear your sarcasm. It would do you well to mind your tongue."

"But then you wouldn't like me half as much." He paused. When she did not respond, he added, "Perhaps if we run? We could see the first one hundred today."

The old countess sighed, and Damen couldn't help but grin. He cared for her with a sort of familial loyalty he couldn't shake. There were certainly other houses not as large, other employers not so demanding, but he couldn't find it in him to leave her. And she paid better than anyone he knew. And of course, there were the other reasons he stayed.

She called over her shoulder, "How's Wellington? Are you supporting him properly?"

This time he sighed.

"Tut! You sound like an old woman, with your sighing."

"Perhaps we would get further in our inspection if Wellington did not need to accompany?" He could hope.

The pug dog draped across his arms, drool wetting his sleeve. He would have to change his jacket as soon as he returned from their walk. A low growl rumbled in Wellington's chest.

The Countess ran a gloved hand along the arm of one of the statues. "He is lovely, is he not?" The man in question stood tall, remembered in white marble.

Damen shook his head. They often came here on their walks, to admire the men who had been immortalized in varying degrees of undress. She had a fine eye for sculpture, the dimension, the expression. But he just saw a room full of shirtless men, or worse.

They continued through the statuary hall to the armory's door. Here was a room he could appreciate. But as if she were trying to torture him, she waved her hand as they walked by. "No one will want to go in there."

He would not argue. The more rooms they skipped the better.

This house party–another one of the countess's eccentric efforts at meddling.

She invited select members of the *ton*, and she prided herself in the vast number of couples who had become affianced in her home. In the past, he had endured the many incessant, simpering demands of the titled and wealthy guests and received little in return.

But not this year. This year, he too would benefit.

Shocking Proposition

No one saw Tabitha standing in the doorway of her brother, Tauney's, room.

James, the valet, lifted clothes *out* of Tauney's trunks in large stacks instead of loading them *in*. Neat, color-coordinated piles of breeches and jackets decorated the bedding, and Tabitha's worry increased.

She shook her head. "We are already so late."

Tauney, only nine months her elder, finished giving animated instructions to James and then waved his hand in her direction. "Late. Psht. The party doesn't even begin for two days."

Of course he would refuse to understand. As the only girl in a family of four brothers, and his closest sibling, she felt responsible for him. She tried another tactic. "If we don't leave now, we will have to delay our journey an extra day and stay at a local inn."

The valet rushed past them, at last packing clothing into Tauney's trunks.

"The local inns. How dreadful." Tauney grimaced. "Do you remember the last time we stayed in one?" His face was so comical, his mouth twisted in disgust. Tabitha couldn't help but laugh.

"But that is exactly my point, though it wasn't so bad."

"For you. My valet had to sleep in the barn. He wasn't even presentable when he came to help me get ready in the morning." His voice lowered to a whisper. "He flicked hay off his person"—Tauney shuddered—"in my presence. It fell to the floor by my foot, and I had to train one eye on it while dressing so as to rid my room of it later." He leaned closer. "Didn't want to hurt his feelings. Good valets are difficult to find, you know."

She often felt pity for his valet.

Her brother was of the opinion that since women spent so many hours concerned with their appearances, they would appreciate the same from men.

Tabitha couldn't argue with that sentiment, especially if they smelled nice. The memory of a distinct earthy aroma warmed her. And she wondered if *he* had arrived. She turned to hide her blush.

She hurried down the stairs. If they were to avoid a war like Napoleon had never seen, she would need to make excuses for Tauney to her other brothers.

The balls on the billiards table cracked and rolled, making her smile. Memories of many a Christmas when their father was still alive, teaching the young Eastons how to play pool, brought a comforting sense of family and home.

She had three of the best men of the *ton* standing right here in her study. And one upstairs, who sometimes had feathers for brains.

"Well, where is he?" Edward, the eldest, frowned.

She laughed, "He has decided on a new color scheme."

When the others groaned, she held up her hand, "But he has promised he is almost finished. I have to admit I am a bit excited to see what he and James accomplish."

"Well I most certainly am not." Edward's frown deepened.

"We promised the countess not to be late. She asked for our particular assistance in helping some of the ladies feel welcome."

Julian humphed. "Of course she did. Trying to hitch us to a woman like all the other mothers in the *ton*. If it wasn't for you, little sister, I would have stayed far away from this house party." As handsome as Julian was, with many women vying for his hand, he naturally felt a bit stifled.

She could well understand the sentiment.

"Come now man, the hunt." Oscar, the fun-loving Corinthian of the bunch, grinned. "You have yet to best me in the hunt." He eyed his next shot. "This will not be the year of course." He sent another ball in a blur across the table and then raised an eyebrow. "But I would think you'd be anxious to try."

Julian took his turn, knocking in all four of the balls. With a satisfied grin, he said,

"This is the year, dear brother."

"Ha-Ha!" Tabitha loved it when they puffed and bristled in fun. "Shall I make a wager?" She won all sorts of money from her brothers, especially when they were pitted against each other.

Julian laughed. "A wager she says! If the matrons could hear you now!"

"We've corrupted her." Edward's eyes held warmth, and she knew a part of him was secretly pleased. "I knew it would happen. What diamond talks as you do?"

Oscar, ever positive, added, "And yet she is a diamond. The books at Whites are filled with their own wagers as to who will win her hand."

Every brother's face went ashen.

She blushed. "It's not as if there is anything to worry about…" But how embarrassing to be discussed in such a manner.

Edward looked positively ill, loosening his cravat, and she began to wonder what had them so concerned.

"What could possibly go wrong?" She looked from face to face. A new sense of foreboding began in the back of her throat in a particular, pointed tightness.

After a silence no one filled, Edward finally said, "It wouldn't hurt for each of you brothers to be looking for wives as well, wealthy ones."

Julian pounded his brother's back. "Always the responsible one." Then he turned to Tabitha. "You are the one we need to focus on this year, Tabby Cat."

"Well, it certainly won't help if you go around addressing me like that."

"Why not? Your *endearing* nickname hasn't turned Henry away."

"Turned me away from what?"

Tabitha's stomach flipped, and she whirled around to face the sixth member of their party.

With a sharp chiseled jawline and eyes sparkling in amusement, Henry filled the doorway. As a dear family friend, most of her childhood memories included Henry. But every time she saw him, a nervous energy coursed through her. She grinned up at him in welcome, but he was looking at Julian.

The brother with the honor of Henry's attention jabbed a thumb in her direction. "Tabby thinks her nickname might not be the thing." He winked.

She dipped her head to hide the blush. "Henry's opinion doesn't count."

"Ho, Ho!" Julian nudged him. "Do you hear that? You don't count."

Henry winked at her. "I suppose she means because I am like a brother? Always present, even when you don't want me." His warm eyes twinkled at her.

She shrugged, looking away. *He will never see. How can I make him see?*

Julian shoved him playfully. "You've heard it often enough, and yet here you are."

"Glutton for punishment." He snatched away the stick and took a turn hitting a ball across the table. "And who says I am here for Tabby? Cook's meat pie can't be beat in any house."

She lifted her chin, suddenly defiant. "Besides, I have no desire to be married."

Laughter filled the room.

"Tabitha Easton, on the shelf."

Oscar shook his head. "That'll never happen."

But Edward moved closer to her, concern on his face. "Ever?"

She sat in the nearest chair. "I suppose it will be a wonderful pastime someday."

"Pastime, she says. *Pastime.*" Julian shook his head. "Let me tell you dear sister. Marriage is like a gentle lead on a new mare. At first she likes the feel. It's soft and nice, appears harmless. But then it pulls tighter and tighter until *ack!*" He demonstrated a noose around the throat with his hands. "It cinches so tight you cannot break away."

A part of her tightened inside like that rope; she wasn't sure why.

Henry cleared his throat, bent down beside her chair, and put his arm across her shoulders.

She felt her neck heat and turned to him, searching his eyes, inches from her own. His expression was playful and full of warmth. She could barely breathe and forced herself to swallow.

"Come now, it isn't as bad as all that." Henry's eyes turned tender. "Let's not ruin it for her."

Before she could stop herself, she leaned closer.

His voice, like a warm breeze, circled around and tickled her insides. "Marriage would be wonderful to the right person, someone to share the thoughts you tell no one else. Your closest friend…"

She smiled and closed her eyes. *Friend.* Would he want such a thing with her? They were friends. Perhaps he was considering it. As she searched his face, nothing seemed different, and yet, there was a new sparkle in his eyes. She grinned in response.

Then the brothers burst into laughter, and her irritation rose. She stood to leave.

Julian rested a hand on Henry's shoulder. "Is that what you do with the women, Henry? Bare your innermost thoughts?"

Oscar looked perplexed. "I don't have innermost thoughts."

"None of us do." Julian's eyes held the tears of laughter. "No wonder Henry can't hang onto a woman."

Tabitha turned in the doorway. "Well, I thought it lovely." She tried to show support as her eyes met Henry's.

His wink sent her insides flipping in funny circles, and she placed a hand on her stomach.

He returned to the table taking a hit at the nearest of three balls, the game forgotten by the others. "Of course she thinks it's lovely, being a woman. I don't expect the rest of your sorry selves to understand."

Oscar snatched the stick. "Whoa there, our sister is not a woman."

Julian laughed. "Oh yes she is! Have you seen her lately?"

She wished to hide beneath the floorboards. And felt so lonely for a sister it nearly caused pain. Ever since her mother had taken ill, she had precious few moments with anyone female she could trust.

"Well, we best get used to the idea." Oscar held up one finger. "Because all the men at this house party are going to notice."

Henry nodded. "Especially when she wears green."

Her face blazed, and she couldn't take any more. "I am right here, you know."

"Then you get to listen in." Edward waved a hand in her direction. "This conversation doesn't require your participation."

Indignation rose. And a great pit of fear opened. Could they have no care for her thoughts?

Oscar stood taller. "Yes. We will review the strategies to keep you protected when we arrive. Only the very worthy shall get past us."

Henry cleared his throat. "Have we decided who she is to marry?"

Tabitha trembled to hear that question spoken so carelessly by his lips. "I believe that

decision is mine." Her voice cracked. She rested a hand on Edward's arm. "These choices are best left in the hands of those they most affect."

Her eldest brother did have sympathy in his eyes, but he said, "It's not really your decision. Father left me in charge of your welfare and wrote in his will how I was to go about ensuring a good and productive marriage arrangement for you."

"We will consider your opinion, of course." Julian's calm tones lessened her mounting discomfort. "But we are all attending this infernal party because we need reinforcements to keep the leeches away."

"Leeches?" This party was sounding more dreadful every moment.

Julian grimaced. "Yes, those undesirables who seek fortune."

Oscar chimed in. "Or that we don't like."

"Or have any sniveling habits. Or can't play cards worth—"

"Or don't know how to hunt a fox." Henry added, moving to stand beside her again.

She loved the surge of tingles that shot through her, as much as she wanted to slink away and hide from them.

"Or any who enjoy battledore." Oscar's calculating expression increased Tabitha's irritation.

They all stopped. Edward asked, "What's wrong with battledore?"

"Oh nothing. I just can't have anyone being overly good at it and beat me at all the family gatherings."

Julian squinted, considering. "You've hit upon something. Shall we have limits on card-playing ability too? We could win money off this chap."

Tabitha said, "Now you are being ridiculous." She was about ready to stomp away. How would she endure an entire carriage ride of the same?

"But truly, sister." Edward gathered all the sticks and balls. "He is to join our family, be one of the brothers. We must make certain he will be a good fit."

"And respect you." Henry's eyes showed deep sympathy. "I too am roped into this. Not all gentlemen behave as a gentleman should. And we are here to make sure you don't have to converse with any of those other sorts."

"I do have a chaperone."

Oscar returned the balls to the table and smacked one into a pocket. "Who? Mrs. Hemming?" He laughed. "She'll be asleep against the wall."

Tabitha was secretly pleased that was the case. All this hovering was beginning to smother her. She moved to leave.

Tauney joined her in the doorway. "Why are you all just sitting around? Let's load the carriage and be off!"

"At last!" Edward put away Oscar's stick. "You are as ridiculous as Prinny with your fashion nonsense."

After an interminable ride in the carriage—and one night in a respectable inn—they at last arrived in front of the Countess du Breven's home in a deluge of rain. The front approach itself took twenty minutes, wheels slogging through wet shale.

And now the great expanse of her lovely house stretched in front of them.

Tabitha lifted the covering over their window to see the approach to the estate. Beech trees lined their entry, limbs bent under the weight of the torrent, but the water brought out a lovely shade of pink in the shale rock of the drive. The whole scene felt otherworldly, and for the first time, a measure of hope rose within her when thinking of the party. "I do love Somerstone Manor." She longed to get lost on the grounds, walking among the flowers and hedges in the countess' expansive gardens.

Mrs. Hemming snored in the corner.

"As long as we can get out of this carriage, I don't care where we stay." Oscar sat stiffly, wedged and jostled against his brothers. Rain pounded the roof, their mounts followed behind. Four broad-shouldered, impatient, and damp men sat pinned together, forced to ride inside once the rain commenced.

They arrived in the hall, shaking water off their persons, the brothers forming a line to Tabitha's front, Henry at her side.

The Countess stepped forward. "We are so happy you have come, Lord Easton." She held out her hand, and Edward bowed over it. The others bowed with him, and Tabitha lowered in a deep curtsey.

Three gentlemen caught Tabitha's eye, coming down the stairs. Anthony Pemberton, one of the Pinkerton twins, and Reginald Beauchamp: three of the most sought after men in the *ton*, all in one place. "Oh. My. I wonder who else the countess has included in her invitations."

Edward followed her gaze and immediately bristled. "Brothers. As soon as we change, let us meet in my room to receive our assignments."

Tabitha sighed.

Henry placed his hand on hers. "Will you be all right? I believe I've been summoned elsewhere."

"Yes, quite." She indicated Mrs. Hemming, who was already bustling her away to get out of her wet things before she caught a chill.

Many eyes watched her move up the stairs. Accustomed to attention, she did not let it rattle her too much. But she would have much preferred a smaller gathering.

Reginald Beauchamp approached on the stairway, flipping his hair away to reveal a brilliant pair of green eyes. She held out her hand. "Hello, Mr. Beauchamp. Pleased to see you again." He was more handsome than any man deserved to be. A pity his attention never focused very long in one direction.

He bowed, and his kiss lingered on her gloved hand.

"Come child. We must get you warmed." Mrs. Hemming scowled at poor Mr. Beauchamp.

He raised his eyebrow in amusement then turned back to Tabitha. "Will I be seeing you at dinner?"

"Yes, she is going to eat, now if you'll excuse us."

"Mrs. Hemming, really." Deep embarrassment filled her. After the discomfort of travel and the slipping sense of control over her life, the emotion almost overwhelmed her. Grasping for something, any decision completely her own, in a moment of pure rebellion, she stepped closer to Mr. Beauchamp, quirked her lips in a half grin.

"Unless you want to meet sooner."

His eyes flew open in shock. Then he recovered, a teasing glint lighting his face.

"You surprise me."

Read the rest HERE for .99

Or FREE by joining her newsletter HERE

Follow Jen

Some of Jen's other published works:

The Nobleman's Daughter
Two lovers in disguise

A Lady's Maid
A dual romance, the struggle continues

Scarlet
The Pimpernel retold

His Lady in Hiding
Hiding out at his maid.

A Foreign Crown
A Lady in Waiting meets a Prince

Spun of Gold
Rumplestilskin Retold

Dating the Duke

Time Travel: Regency man in NYC

Tabitha's Folly
Four over protective Brothers

To read Damen's Secret
The Villain's Romance

Charmed by His Lordship
A fake alliance

Follow her Newsletter

About the Author

An award winning author, including the GOLD in Foreword INDIES Book of the Year Awards, Jen Geigle Johnson discovered her passion for England while kayaking on the Thames near London as a young teenager.

She once greeted an ancient turtle under the water by grabbing her fin. She knows all about the sound a water-ski makes on glassy water and how to fall down steep moguls with grace. During a study break date in college, she sat on top of a jeep's roll bars up in the mountains and fell in love.

Now, she loves to share bits of history that might otherwise be forgotten. Whether in Regency England, the French Revolution, or Colonial America, her romance novels are much like life is supposed to be: full of adventure. She is a member of the RWA, the SCBWI, and LDStorymakers. She is also the chair of the Lonestar.Ink writing conference.

Follow her Newsletter HERE.

https://www.jengeiglejohnson.com

Twitter--@authorjen

Instagram--@authorlyjen